## FROM WARM WOMEN
## TO COLD FURY

Longarm stroked her gently until he felt her hips begin to move with him. Her breath was coming in short, quick gasps, and she began to knead the firm muscles of his back.

Birgita's neck arched and her body quivered. Then she bit her lip as she stifled a cry of pleasure. She nuzzled his neck.

Suddenly, a thought exploded in Longarm's brain. He sat bolt upright. "Son of a bitch!" he swore angrily. "If only it had come to me before. Your friend Randy is wanted in Texas for suspicion of murder. And I let him walk away!"

## TABOR EVANS

# LONGARM

## AND THE BUCKSKIN ROGUE

A JOVE BOOK

LONGARM AND THE BUCKSKIN ROGUE

A Jove Book / published by arrangement with
the author

PRINTING HISTORY
Jove edition / March 1983

ISBN: 0-515-06254-5

Jove books are published by Jove Publications, Inc.,
200 Madison Avenue, New York, N.Y. 10016. The words
"A JOVE BOOK" and the "J" with sunburst are trademarks
belonging to Jove Publications, Inc.

PRINTED IN THE UNITED STATES OF AMERICA

# Chapter 1

Longarm reached back to stand his pillow on end and bunch it at the back of his neck. He gave a long, slow sigh of sheer contentment as he reached past the Colt hanging on his bedpost to find a cheroot and a sulphur-tipped match. He flicked the match to flame with his thumbnail, drew on the cigar until he had a satisfactory coal alight, and shook the match out.

"Here," a soft voice said. A slender arm snaked out from under the sheet, found a saucer on the bedside table, and handed it to him. "I cannot abide the sight of ashes on bedding," she said.

Longarm set the saucer on his lightly sweat-filmed belly, and tapped a thin circlet of pale gray ash onto the plate. "I thought you were asleep," he said gently.

"In a dream perhaps, but not asleep."

"That sounds like a compliment, ma'am."

"It was, sir." She lifted her head from the crook of his arm where she had been resting and gave him an impish look. "Would you be willing to prove to me once again that you are deserving of my compliments?"

Longarm chuckled, and the saucer bounced on the hard, flat slabs of muscle above his waistline. "I'll do my best to prove it, ma'am. I'm just a poor old country boy with a badge pinned to his chest."

She giggled. "Where?"

"There." Longarm pointed.

The girl shifted on top of him and began to lick his chest. "Nope," she said, "can't find it. It must be down here." She disappeared beneath the sheet that covered him to his waist, but that hardly kept him from being aware of what she was up to. He became aware too that he might be up to more than he really expected of himself after a full Saturday night and a delightful Sunday as well.

"Oh my," she said with an exclamation of mock surprise. "Is *this* your badge?"

"Close enough," Longarm said. He laid the saucer and cheroot aside and reached for her, intending to draw her up to where he might be able to return the favor, but he was interrupted by a loud knocking at the door.

"Some son of a bitch better have an awful good reason for this," Longarm said as he swung his bare, knobby legs off the side of the bed and stood upright for the first time in hours. Pulling on his trousers, he told the girl, "You have two choices, I reckon. Put on enough clothes to pass as being halfway respectable, or hide."

"Hide? Why, I've never . . . but oh my, what a marvelous tale to tell Lucy when I get home." She laughed. "I have never had occasion to hide in a gentleman's bedchamber, Marshal Long. I simply *must* do it. Under the bed is traditional, is it not?"

"So I've heard," Longarm said with a chuckle.

The knocking sounded again, louder and more insistent

this time. "I'm coming. Just a minute," Longarm called.

The girl stifled a case of the giggles, took the sensible precaution of removing the sheet from the bed and wrapping it around herself, then dropped to all fours and wriggled underneath Longarm's sagging bed.

The sight of her white-swathed rump swaying back and forth as she scuttled out of sight was intriguing, and Longarm thought it might be something worth remembering and returning to later.

For the moment, though, he was curious about who would have poor enough manners to disturb a fellow's peaceful Sunday afternoon. Barefoot and clad only in his stovepipe trousers, he picked up his Colt and went to stand at the side of the door while he snatched it open with an unexpected speed calculated to unnerve whoever was there. Sunday afternoon or no, there was no point in being lazily foolish— or maybe lazily dead.

The gaping muzzle of Longarm's .44 caliber Colt greeted the pink, smiling face of Federal Marshal Billy Vail. Billy looked totally unperturbed by the abrupt greeting. But then, he had received it before.

"Afternoon, Longarm," Billy said politely. "Mind if I come in?"

"Damn it, Billy, as a matter of fact I *do* mind."

But it was already too late. Vail was inside the room and making for the dressing table, where a bottle of Maryland rye sat in plain sight. He found two glasses in a reasonable state of cleanliness and raised the bottle toward Longarm in a small salute of sorts. "Shall I pour for you too?"

Longarm shrugged and bit back a cussword. He accepted the inevitable and closed his door, returning his Colt to its holster on the bedpost and accepting the drink of his own liquor offered by his own boss.

"Sit down, Longarm. You needn't be formal here," Billy said with a gesture toward the straight-backed chair that sat in a corner. Vail himself perched on the side of Longarm's bed.

Longarm winced. He wondered if that was giggling he

3

was hearing or if it was his own imagination.

Damn it, if there was anyone the chief marshal would not want to find one of his deputies cavorting with, it was that pretty little thing under Custis Long's rumpled bed. Her daddy happened to be a United States congressman who held a senior seat on the budget committee. She had been passing through Denver on her way to the summer nabob colony down at Colorado Springs when she decided to go slumming in the arms of a tall, handsome deputy marshal.

At the time, even after he found out who she was, it had seemed a fine idea. After all, a man should not hold it against a girl just because she was wealthy and beautiful and talented in bed.

Now, with Billy Vail's heels raising the dust to tickle her nose under this particular deputy's bed, it did not seem like such a marvelous notion after all.

Longarm groaned and fortified himself with a jolt of Maryland rye. "I hope you have a good reason for dropping by on a Sunday afternoon, Billy, or I just might find a reason to throw you out."

Vail grinned at him, and once again Longarm was reminded that there were worse men he could have been working under in the Justice Department. He had known more than one chief marshal who would have had him up on charges of insubordination for a remark like that one. Unlike some, though, Vail was no carryover from the Grant Administration, when political clout was all that mattered and professional expertise be damned. Billy had done his share of rough work with a gun in his hand and sweat in his eyes, and he knew what it was like for his deputies when they were in the field. Longarm fondly hoped the old devil would live forever.

He also suspected that Billy Vail was fully aware of his deputy's discomfort of the moment and was thoroughly enjoying it.

"Official business, Longarm. You know I wouldn't think of disturbing you otherwise." Billy took a sip of rye.

Longarm decided to let that pass. Understanding or not,

the boss should not often be told by his deputy that he is a liar.

"Actually," Vail went on, "I was dragged away from my own weekend pursuits, and if it is important enough to take me from my guests it should be important enough to take you from—uh—whatever you were doing." A bushy eyebrow rose, reminding Longarm of a caterpillar crawling up a bare rock.

"Just resting," Longarm said easily.

"Good. No harm done, then." Billy took another drink of Longarm's Maryland rye.

"Uh-huh." A half-blind, three-quarters-drunk saloon swamper could not have missed all the female finery draped and dropped throughout Longarm's room, of course, but if Billy did not want to mention it, Longarm was not going to. "So tell me what's so damned important that you have to interrupt my nap," he went on.

"All right, Deputy." The use of the title instead of his nickname told Longarm that playtime was over and the marshal was about to get down to business. "We have been asked to do a favor for Interior. They're having a spot of trouble, practically at our own back door."

Longarm groaned. "Don't tell me some fool Indian agent..."

"Calm down, now. You needn't get excited. They just want you to pop 'round and shoot a horse for them. It has nothing to do with Indians this time." Vail took another sip of the excellent rye.

"Shoot a *horse?* Good Lord, Billy, they..."

"And while you're at it," Vail went on blandly, "you might inquire about why someone has been murdering the Federal game control agents who were sent out to do that same simple job."

Now it was Longarm's turn to raise his eyebrows. He reached for a cheroot and a match. He suspected, rightly, that Billy Vail was going to require a little time to expand upon that statement.

\* \* \*

When Vail finally took a break to moisten his dry throat with another glass of Longarm's rye, Longarm leaned back in his chair to chew on the stub of his cigar while he thought over what Billy had just told him.

It was no secret that the Bureau of Land Management hired predator control hunters to keep the public lands reasonably clear of predators for the benefit of the stockmen who grazed those lands. In addition to their salaries, the hunters generally collected state and county bounties for the scalps and ears or tails of coyotes, mountain lions, bears, eagles, and very nearly any other species of wildlife suspected of causing depredation among the calves, foals, and lambs.

Longarm's personal impression was that most stockmen were a little too quick to accuse. It was always easier to blame stock loss on some wily predator than for a man to admit his own stupidity when it came to winter-kill or lack of nourishment for some hardscrabble farmer's livestock. As a result, any dead lamb meant a hue and cry for every coyote within twenty miles, and the resulting bounties meant money in someone's pocket for every eagle carcass brought to earth.

Longarm thought the whole thing was about as sensible as building baskets out of buffalo chips. But then, no one had asked his opinion, And the fact remained that those hunters were technically Federal employees, just like himself.

Now it seemed that someone had taken upon himself the task of ridding the grasslands of game control agents, just as those hunters were supposed to be ridding the area of coyotes. Or, in this case, ridding a particular area of a particular horse.

The last two control officers sent out with instructions to kill this rogue buckskin stud were found face down and fish-belly cold, with bullets in their backs.

"The first murder frankly didn't cause all that much excitement," Billy had told him. "There were no witnesses, of course, but a man can find all sorts of ways to get himself

6

shot. An argument, mistaken identity—anything could have happened. No one even knew for sure whether the first hunter had finished his job before he was killed.

"So George Seemus—he's the one running the program here—waited until he received some more complaints about the rogue stallion before he assigned another hunter to it. Seemus is the one who dragged me away from home this afternoon. He's feeling guilty about assigning a second man and sending him out to get shot without any suspicion that the man might be in danger. He's really rattled about it.

"Anyway, yesterday afternoon some cowboys found the second hunter backshot on the open grass southeast of Castle Rock. They hauled him over to the railroad and sent his body north. Seemus got the package today and has been noisily falling apart ever since. He sent some wires to Washington and apparently he has enough political connections to get his answers back on a Sunday afternoon. Including a wire from Justice instructing me—us, I should say—to take an interest in the murders of the two game control agents.

"We have damned little to go on, actually. Both men were operating in the same general area and both were assigned to shoot the same buckskin stallion. And both are now dead."

Billy shifted on the side of the bed and took another drink. "The only thing we can safely assume is that the horse isn't the one who shot them. Beyond that..." He shrugged. "Damned if I know what's beyond that."

Vail reached into his coat pocket and brought out a small, flat envelope and a gauze-wrapped packet. "These are the only clues we have to go on."

The envelope contained a cracking, yellowed photographic portrait of the kind that were taken at some county fairs or other festive gatherings by roving photographers. It showed a trio of big-hatted, smiling cowboys mounted on saddle horses and with their catch ropes in their hands, loops formed and posing as if they were all three about to rope the photographer.

7

"The one you are interested in," Billy said, "is the horse on the right in that picture. You needn't bother with the man. The horse stomped him to death and ran off the day he went wild and took to killing people."

"People?" Longarm asked. "He's killed others, then?"

Billy nodded. "Two that we know of. They also say he steals cattle, but I wouldn't know anything about that. The point is, we've been asked to put a bullet in his brisket. Seemus is understandably reluctant to assign another man."

Longarm nodded, returned the print to its envelope, and tossed it onto the bedside table to study more closely later. "And the other evidence there?"

Vail handed it to him. It was a bullet. The gauze it had been wrapped in showed traces of dark and long-dry blood and the shattered, mushroomed nose of the projectile showed bits of gore as well. Longarm had little doubt about where the bullet had come from. What interested him was its peculiar construction.

"Odd, ain't it?"

Vail nodded. "I'm not sure what it is."

"That makes a pair of us," Longarm said.

"Practically no rifling marks on the base there where it isn't deformed. Which means it is a patched ball, most likely. Try to scratch it with your thumbnail."

Longarm did. He was able to achieve a slight mark in the surface coloration of the metal, but his nail left no real impression. "Damn, that's hard. There's a powerful amount of antimony in the lead." He lit another cheroot and stared toward the ceiling in thought. "A lot of buffalo hunters with Sharps or Remington Long Toms will patch their bullets. And of course a Creedmore type shooter will patch. But all of 'em I've ever seen mold their slugs with plain old general store lead. They don't go to the trouble and the expense of dressing it up to that kind of hardness without a good reason." He shook his head. "I don't know, Billy. That's one damn strange bullet. I've never seen one like it before."

"Exactly," Vail said. "If you want to keep it, all right; but, if you don't, I might spend some time trying to figure out what it is and what kind of rifle it came from."

"It could help if you do," Longarm agreed. He wrapped the mangled slug back in the gauze and handed it to his boss.

"In the meantime," Vail said, "I'd suggest you wander down that way and make a show of going after the buckskin rogue. If there's any connection between the horse and the murders, that might drive the murderer out into the open."

Longarm looked at him and grinned. "You know, Billy, if that's some kind of newfangled bullet out of some kind of newfangled gun that lets a man shoot from ambush at a mile away an' never miss his mark, why, I don't think I'm ever gonna forgive you for using me as bait."

"That seems fair," Vail said, rising from the side of Longarm's bed. "I guess I'll just have to take my chances."

"Do that, Billy."

Longarm walked with him to the door. As Vail reached the entryway he paused. Without turning his head he said over his shoulder, "Nice to've met you, Miss."

"My pleasure, I'm sure." The girl sounded like she was strangling from trying to speak and giggle at the same time.

Longarm shrugged. "I'll get on this in the morning."

"You do that, Deputy. You just do that little thing."

Longarm shut the door with Billy Vail on the other side of it and turned to enjoy the show as a dusty but obviously delighted young lady crawled on her belly out from under his bed.

"You're a terrible housekeeper," she accused, brushing herself off. "There are dust balls down there."

"Housekeeping is not what I'm famous for," he said.

She smiled. "Prove it."

# Chapter 2

Longarm paid off the driver of the hack, made a mental note of the amount so he would remember to put it on his expense sheet, and snorted as a shift of gusty wind sent the decidedly earthy scent of the Denver stockyards washing over him.

A man could get used to living without that kind of shit—easily—he reflected.

On the other hand, there were some pretty good boys working around this maze of pens and chutes and runs and bawling, manure-fouled cattle. And some of those boys might have some answers for him. Billy had said that this was where the rogue stallion had killed its owner, and this was the place it had run away from. If he was after the buckskin, as he at least partially was, this was as good a place as any to start.

Longarm settled his Stetson more firmly on his head and ignored the muck that was getting on his boots as he strode toward a group of cowhands working a pen of mixed stock.

As he came closer to the cowhands, Longarm recognized a couple of familiar faces among the loafers perched on the top rail watching the others work. Longarm climbed up to join them.

"Well, if it ain't the long arm of the law come to admire us workin' folk," said one of the cowhands.

"Howdy, Dave, Petey. How are you boys gettin' along?" He nodded to the men he did not know and pulled a cheroot from his vest pocket.

"Not nowheres near enough is what we're gettin'," Petey said.

Dave reached across Longarm to help himself to one of the lawman's cheroots, then struck a match and lighted up for both of them.

"Nice of you," Longarm observed. "If you want, you can lay down in that cow plop there. I'll jump onto your chest to get the air moving for you, save you the trouble of doing it yourself."

"Thanks, but I don't want to get my spurs clogged with mud."

Longarm nodded solemnly. The bent and rusty nubbins that Dave was using for spurs had long since lost their rowels and probably should have been thrown away as useless even before that, but Dave had been wearing the same twisted bits of prod steel for as long as Longarm had known him around the saloons of Denver.

They sat for a time in silence, smoking and observing the activity in the pen in front of them. A mixed herd wearing an FR Connected Bar was being sorted by two hands on cutting horses, steers down one runway and cows into another. There were no calves in the group. Gatemen and a group of youngsters with prod poles kept the animals moving once they were sorted into the proper alleys. The steers

11

would bring a higher price than the canners, but eventually each group would find its way onto a succession of tables.

The work was slow but hardly dull for anyone with an appreciation of what was being done. The cutting horses moved for the most part with deliberation, easing a chosen animal out of the herd and to its appointed place without exciting any of the other bovines. Only when one of the cattle tried to bolt back into the herd did the horses pin their ears and dart into a flurry of activity to block the bovine's charge and force it away from where it wanted to be.

When that happened a flying hoof would sometimes send a stream of hot, fresh manure curling into the air. And when one of those found a resting place on the neck or chest of a cowboy there was an instant and cheerful response from the idlers who were watching. There was just no way to cut cattle in a stockyard pen without coming out looking like you had been wallowing on the ground instead of riding a horse.

"So how're things down at the Diamond K?" Longarm asked after a considerable period of neighborly silence had gone by.

"Aw, you know how it is. Gets so boring a man don't hardly know what to do with himself. We didn't have anything better to do, so we come up here to keep from stretching our bunk ropes any further. Petey's there is fixin' to touch the floor if he don't quit layin' in it so much."

Longarm nodded. "I've heard you boys have it that way. Boredom's the reason I was driven to honest work myself."

The truth was—and Longarm knew it—there was little work that was harder and practically none that was poorer paid than a cowhand's. For thirty dollars a month—half that in some places and at some times—they were expected to be up early enough to eat and be on the job, which might start twenty miles from their bedrolls, by the time the sun showed itself over the horizon. They worked until the job was done, which was never likely to be a minute before sundown and was often later, and still rode night herd for part of the night.

They ate poorly, were expected to get a day's work out of any raunchy bronc that was dumped into their string, and would have been shunned as slackers if they failed to take everything that came their way with cheerful good humor. Yet they were among the proudest and most independent men Longarm had ever known.

The poor bastards simply didn't know how bad they had it, Longarm had decided long ago. They took everything rank horses, wild cattle, and miserable weather could dish out at them and came back for more. They were all undeniably crazy by any civilized accounting, but they didn't seem to know that either.

"I got something here you boys might be able to tell me about," Longarm said after another silence. He reached inside his vest and pulled out the picture Vail had given him. "See anything familiar there?"

The Diamond K hands bent over the picture, but it required only a moment for Petey to break into a grin and begin showing it around to the other loafers.

"That there's ol' Buck an' Lew Chance that used to own him," Petey said, with more animation on his nearly toothless features than Longarm could remember seeing there before. "Son of a bitch if it ain't. An' those other boys— I don't know their names, but I've seen them around time to time. A while back, this woulda been, though. Lew's been dead a spell now. Fact is, it was old Buck that kilt him. Right over there near the pens." He pointed vaguely beyond the stockyards.

"Killed him, huh?" Longarm asked, letting Petey take the bait and run with it without feeling that he was being questioned by an officer of the law.

"Jeez, yes. Listen, this horse you got a picture of right here; well, you see that sorrel over there?" He aimed his chin toward the better of the two cutting horses working in the pen.

Longarm nodded. "I've been enjoying watching him work."

"Well, you ain't seen a horse work yet if you think that

one's good. He don't know cow from coonskin compared to ol' Buck. That Buck was the best damn cuttin' horse I ever seen. An' I've seen a heap of 'em in my time, you can believe it."

Another hand, drawn by the mention of the horse's name, leaned closer and said. "He's tellin' you the natural truth. There never was a horse could work cow better than that Buck. It was a privilege just to see him at his trade."

Off to the right, yet another of the loafers joined in. "I've *rode* that horse, boys, and I tell you I'll never ride a better. Point him t' the one you want an' turn loose o' the reins. That's all it took. He'd do all the rest. Never had to touch him with rein nor spur, either one. Just point him in the direction and leave him be."

Petey snorted. "That's 'bout all that damned ol' Lew could do with him too. He was always so near drunk it's a wonder he didn't fall outa the saddle just settin' still. Buck had all the sense for both of them."

"Bastard knew it, too," a cowboy on Longarm's left said. "That's likely why he abused the horse so bad."

"If it'd been my animal he treated like that," another one said, "I'd of taken a club to old Lew's head. Son of a bitch had the best horse in the country, but he'd get all likkered up and kill his snakes by beating that horse. The only wonder is that the horse never kilt him before it finally did."

"I don't know," another cut in. "A horse won't hardly ever take after a man no matter what you do to it 'less it's a born man-killer anyhow. Which I hear this Buck damn sure is. They say he's killed seven, maybe eight boys down south of here. And there's plenty can testify they seen him kill Lew. Plenty more since him, too."

Men Longarm had hardly noticed before were crowding around now to join into the conversation. It seemed that he had touched a nerve when he brought up the subject of the buckskin rogue and its deceased owner, Lew Chance.

"The son of a bitch is a man-killer, all right," one of them said, "but he's got so much cow in him he keeps on workin' them even now that he's gone wild. Steals them,

14

he does. Not that I figure a horse knows shit about stealin'. What I mean, he's still workin' cows when he comes across them. There's boys down south of here that've had cows stole by this Buck, but nobody knows where he takes them afterward. Must have him a mess of them tucked away somewheres by now."

"Maybe he just drifts them way the hell and gone somewhere an' when they drift they go off so far the brand book don't show them as legal owned anywhere, so they're sold at sheriff's auctions if they're ever picked up by anybody."

That, Longarm thought, was the most sensible suggestion he had heard yet about how a feral horse would go about stealing cattle from honest stockmen. He was at least willing to think about it as a possibility. It might pay to send some wires to brand inspectors in Kansas and the Staked Plains areas just to make sure.

"This Buck, though," Petey was persisting. "Gawd, he could cut cattle. I never seen him slip one. Worked with his ol' nose right down in the dirt. Head an' neck whipping around like a snake. A cow tried to run under him to get by, I've seen him draw blood with his teeth, he'd bite them so hard. He'd do any damn thing to turn a cow."

"Bite them? I've seen horses do that before. Stud horses use their teeth a good bit anyhow." The man rubbed his shoulder and grimaced. "It ain't fun to get bit by a stud horse."

"It wasn't no damn teeth that got old Lew," another man said.

"No, sir," Dave agreed.

"What did happen, then?" Longarm prodded.

"I guess you wasn't here, was you? Old Lew, he was drunk as usual that day, but mebbe more so. He got hisself a belly plumb full, beat the shit outa the horse, and then went to ride him. I guess the horse had had about enough. Buck was smarter'n Lew anyhow. What he done was to lope off like he was just going to be fine in spite of the beating he'd just took. Lew got hisself relaxed in the saddle, and old Buck pitched him cloud-high. Set in to squealing and bellering—you know how a stud horse can do. Bucking like he was still trying to throw Lew after the son of a bitch was already ten feet in the air. When Lew hit the ground that horse's front hoofs come down plumb on his noggin. Cracked his head open like a melon."

"Lew didn't have no brains, but he sure had a lot of mess in his skull," someone else said.

One of the men shivered just from the memory of it. It had damn sure made an impression on those who saw it.

"Anyway, Lew was dead right off. He sure as hell didn't linger an' suffer none. Buck took off to the south, right across that flat down there, an' over the hills, still bucking and kicking and hollering for as long as any of us seen him."

"That's my last sight o' that horse. Pitchin' for all he was worth an' them stirrups flappin' and Lew layin' dead on the ground behind him."

"By the time any of us could get over there, Buck was long gone an' Lew was long dead. Haven't seen the horse since."

"Sure heard about him, though. Killin' people. Stealin' cows. Who knows what all, or why."

"Gone loco. Purely loco," someone offered as an explanation.

"He was a helluva horse in his time, though."

"Best I ever seen."

"Best I ever expect to see. There just couldn't be a better."

The excitement in their voices and on their faces died away as the men thought about the loco cutting horse and perhaps about the man who had owned him. They were silent.

"A horse like that," Longarm said quietly, "I'm kinda looking forward to seeing him."

"Seein' him? You goin' after him?" Petey asked.

"I've been asked to," Longarm said. "It's strange as hell, but the law wants him dead. They told me to go find him."

"Son of a bitch," someone mumbled. "Don't know as I'd want to see the old boy put down."

16

"You would if it was your cattle he was carrying off," someone else said.

"I reckon."

There was a collective sigh as the men thought about the demise of the grand old outlaw. Longarm was not sure that he disagreed with them, either.

"You headed south, Longarm?" Dave asked. "That's where we heard he's been using."

"Uh-huh."

"Got to rent you a horse down there?"

"Either that or get one from the remount." Longarm made a face. "I'm sure tired of those long-legged, stupid sons they always palm off on me."

Dave grinned. "It just so happens I got a decent five-year-old gelding wearing my own brand that I've sold to a feller down that way. I—uh—got no hankering to pay to ship him. You could take him, use him as long as you need, an' then deliver him to a fella named Troy Foster down by Fountain."

"Decent horse?" Longarm asked.

Dave looked wounded. "Didn't I break him out my own self? Didn't I raise him from a pup? Didn't I gentle him so pretty a schoolmarm could go Sunday ridin' on him? That ain't no question to ask, Longarm."

Longarm grinned. "That bad, huh? What the hell. I owe you a favor for helping me get rid of my cigars."

That solved Longarm's problem of horseflesh for the near future. It seemed like it was getting harder and harder to get a decent mount for non-Army use out of the boys at remount. And the truth was that Dave was quite a hand. If he had broken the horse out, it would be trained right.

"Trot the rascal out," Longarm said. "I'll see that he finds his way home sometime."

"I don't suppose . . ."

"No, I don't suppose I could put through a voucher for rental on him. I'd get chewed out for certain sure if I rented a horse out of Denver when I could as easy take a remount

17

nag. So don't push your luck."

Dave grinned at him. "It was worth the try."

"It was," Longarm agreed. Now all he had to do was get down south and hope someone took a shot at him.

*Simple, right?* he asked himself. *Right.*

If only he believed that.

But he had no better ideas. He climbed down off the rails and reached for a cheroot. That was another thing. He had to remember to pick up some more cigars and a bottle or two before he left. You never knew what you might not be able to find once you got beyond the civilized environs of the big city.

He hitched up his pants and set off behind Dave to find that borrowed horse.

At least this case was starting off all right.

# Chapter 3

The young deputy assigned by the Elbert County sheriff to show Longarm to the scene of the second murder turned out to be a pleasant enough youngster. They rode side by side at a comfortable road jog south and east from Castle Rock.

"We sure were happy to hear that the gov'ment was sending a hunter in to kill that damn stud horse," he said. "That buckskin rogue has caused us no end o' trouble around here. In other counties too."

"For instance?" Longarm prompted.

"Stealing cattle, mostly," the kid said. His name was Jasper, but that had somehow been translated into Jaybird over the years, and he'd invited Longarm to call him that, the same as everyone else did. "Not big herds or anything like that. He'll come onto a herd and cut out just a few head at a time. Three or four, maybe. Not often more than that. And he'll just drift them off to wherever he goes with them. It's for sure nobody ever found the place."

"That doesn't seem like much of a loss to get excited about, Jaybird. Why all the fuss?"

The kid gave Longarm a sideways glance and coughed into his fist before he answered. He seemed more embarrassed than pleased to know something that this well known deputy United States marshal didn't, and Longarm found himself liking Jaybird for that.

"The thing is, sir..."

"Longarm to my friends, Jaybird," he corrected with a smile.

"Yes, sir. I mean, Longarm. Anyway, the folks that have been losing these little bitty bands of cattle ain't the big operators like you have further out on the plains or up in Wyoming or even down below Pueblo. Along the Front Range here we've mostly got a bunch of small operators. Good folks, mind, and proud. They just ain't rich. Mostly there'll be a family with a cabin or a soddy at the home place, a garden for the woman an' kids to tend and a few head of cattle. Some of them are trying dry-land farming still, but most have already given up on that. There's a colony of Germans not too far from here and a bunch of Rooshians on south. Some Irish and what-have-you. You know—folks."

Longarm nodded.

"Anyhow, these folks got little enough to start with. Losing three cows wouldn't mean a thing to Prent Olive or one of them big foreign outfits you read about in the papers. But three cows is half of some folks' herd down this way."

Jaybird chuckled, and Longarm cranked his eyebrows up. "What were you thinking just then?"

"Oh, them Rooshians. I heard tell that some of them bought rangy old Longhorn cattle like most of them still are around here and then set in to milking them. I was just

20

thinking it'd be worth a ride down there just to see it."

Longarm grinned. The idea of a farmer trying to milk a pint out of a slab-sided, leggy old Texas mama tickled him too. It should be a hell of a fight and fun to watch if not to join in on. "You were telling me about the buckskin rogue," he reminded Jaybird.

"Yeah. Well, he comes around pretty regular, like I said. He's a real bother to folks."

"You ever see him?"

"No, I never seen him myself, exactly. Seen his tracks, of course, but that's as close as I come to him. Wouldn't need a gov'ment hunter down here if I did get a look at him."

"How about the people who have lost stock to him?"

Jaybird scratched his chin and thought for a moment before he answered. "Mostly he comes at night, they say. Not many have laid eyes on him. There's a lady on south..." He shook his head. "I disremember exactly. Heard something about it but I don't recall what."

"What about the hunter?"

"That I know more about. He hadn't checked in with the sheriff the way you done—him not bein' a lawman or anything like that—but we knew he was in the area. Seen him a time or two at breakfast. Big ol' fella with a coat that smelled worse than a Kansas City feedlot. Looked like he knew what he was doing too. He was a hunter, though, not a gunman. Carried a big old Sharps with at least a fifteen-pound octagon barrel, but didn't own a belly gun. At least we didn't find any on him or in his gear, nor any cartridges nor fixings for a short gun. He had a bunch of traps packed onto a mule that he'd left in town when he went hunting for this horse.

"Anyway, he went off as usual and we never thought a thing about him not coming back to the livery. Figured a hunter would be likely to stay out as long as he needed, and the moon was full enough last week to spot movement a long ways out on the grass. Then Saturday evening Bobby Dewell came fogging it into town with his horse lathered

21

up. Bobby and his daddy had been out looking for some fresh antelope meat and come across the body. I was one that came out to fetch him back to town, which is why I know where to take you." Jaybird tipped his hat back. "Maybe you could answer me a question, Longarm."

"Maybe," Longarm agreed.

"It don't seem right that a man should be shot down in my jurisdiction here and me not even know the poor bastard's right name. Wolf is all we heard, but that's just a nickname, I guess."

"Murder bothers you, does it?"

"I reckon that it does."

"Good. Long as a man's dying bothers you, Jaybird, you'll make a fine lawman. You have the makings to be a good one. If you don't let yourself get so that innocent people's hurting *doesn't* vex you, why, you'll be all right."

Jaybird looked pleased with the compliment.

"As for your question, you heard the man's name right," Longarm went on. "It's spelled with an 'e'. Charles Wolfe. He'd been out here long enough to have trapped beaver with Bridger and Fitzpatrick and those boys."

"Seems a waste, don't it?"

"Uh-huh. And a puzzlement too about how a bush-whacker could get close enough to a man like that to drop him after he'd been able to survive when the Blackfoot and Gros Ventres were raising hell. That's a puzzlement indeed."

They topped another of the endless successions of rises that formed this part of the country and Jaybird pulled his horse to a stop. He pointed to an empty stretch of grass that would have taken someone familiar with the country to recognize as distinct from any other and said, "Right down there is where they found him."

"I expect the area is pretty well trampled over after taking him out," Longarm said.

"Not as bad as you might think. We ain't entirely rubes out here."

"Sorry."

"What we done, we made sure we come in along the same path that the Dewells used when they first found him. And the Dewells aren't slouches. They'd already checked around the body for tracks and found none. Personally I'd trust them. Pop Dewell has been here a while too and he knows what he's doing. Whoever shot Mr. Wolfe never came up to the body afterward."

"Did you find the place where the shot came from?"

"No. We left our horses by the body and walked a circle a hundred fifty yards out or thereabouts but we never found anything. We had to come back Sunday morning to do that, as it was already coming dark when we got to the body."

Longarm nodded. He sat with his reins slack and lit a cheroot while he studied the scene below. He could see the beaten grass where the body had been. From the rise they were sitting on it was at least six hundred yards away. Much too far for an effective rifle shot, regardless of what the braggarts and liars might claim. Beyond the depression where the body had been found and perhaps another quarter mile away there was another rise. "We'll take a look up there," he said, pointing.

"Awful long shot," Jaybird noted.

"If you have a better idea I'll listen to it."

"No, sir. I mean, Longarm."

They jogged the horses across, ignoring the place where Wolfe's body had been found.

"Could have been here," Longarm said eventually. He pointed. There was a small patch of grass that had been pressed against the ground and had not recovered. But the summer-dry, brown prairie grasses at this time of year would have practically no recovery once they were disturbed. A man could have lain there on Saturday to shoot Charles Wolfe. Or an antelope might have bedded there for an afternoon nap two weeks earlier. There were no tracks in the hard, dry soil to tell either way. There was also a rock nearby that could have been used by a bushwhacker to rest the barrel of his rifle while he made a quarter-mile shot from a prone position. It might as easily have been just

23

another rock. There simply was no way to tell.

"It sure would be easier," Longarm said, "if killers would learn to leave business cards behind. Even an empty cartridge case would help." He reached behind and pulled a bottle of Maryland rye from his right-hand saddlebag. "Care for a swallow?"

"No, thank you. Uh, is that all? That's all we come out here for, Longarm?" Jaybird looked disappointed.

Longarm took a swallow, recorked the bottle, and returned it to his saddlebag. He shrugged. "We rode out here just in case the bushwhacker was a complete idiot, son, which it looks like he ain't. I didn't really expect him to be or you'd already have solved this thing without my help. What it comes down to, county or Federal, a lawman has to nibble his apple one small bite at a time and just keep going until he gets it all done." He pulled his horse around. "I reckon we can start back any time you're ready."

"But we didn't learn anything."

"Not so, Jaybird. I got a feeling in my gut that we're right now at the place the killer fired from. Could be wrong, of course, but I don't think so. So what we've learned is that our bushwhacker—whoever he is and for whatever reason he shot—is one hell of a good man with a rifle. Because that right there, long as it is and shooting downhill, that right there is one hell of a piece of marksmanship.

"We also learned that he picked up his brass. Could be a professional shooter, either of animals or of men. Buffalo hunter or hired assassin, either one will pick up his empty brass when he's done. So I reckon this ride has told us a thing or two after all."

Jaybird looked somewhat happier to learn that he might have actually helped the tall deputy marshal. He heeled his horse forward and led the way back toward the Castle Rock.

Longarm brushed past the hanging strings of beads, a futile attempt to discourage flies, and crossed the sawdust-littered floor to the end of the bar away from the free lunch. After a supper of fried steak and fried potatoes smothered in gravy

24

he felt no inclination to load up on the cold offerings on the counter. He ordered Maryland rye and told the bartender to leave the bottle.

Standing at the end of the bar with one elbow on the unpolished surface, he had a wall at his back and a decent view of most of the room.

The saloon was not exceptionally busy, but there was a steady flow of customers. Most of the tables were filled, either with men having a drink and conversation after a day's work or with quieter and much more intent card players. There were no fancy roulette wheels or such professional gambling devices in evidence here, and the one girl who was working the place accepted a slow shake of Longarm's head as a refusal without pushing the issue.

"Anything else, mister?" the bartender asked. "Peanuts maybe, or..."

He was interrupted by the rising voices that suddenly came from one of the tables, where four men were bent over a game of stud poker.

"Cheating son of a bitch!" someone yelled. The man, sitting with his back toward the bar, half rose in his seat.

"Sit down and play, fer cryin' out loud. Bad luck ain't the same as a cheat," another of the players said in a bored tone.

"Excuse me," the bartender muttered to Longarm. He began an unhurried stroll toward the open end of the bar.

"I seen him cheat me," the first man protested loudly. "I seen him."

"Pipe down, Nate. Nobody has to cheat to beat you."

Nate stood up to loom menacingly above the other three players, and Longarm cocked his head and eyed the man with professional interest. Still, as long as it turned out to be a fair fight it was really none of his business.

The bartender increased his walking speed by a bit, Longarm noticed. He was nearing the table now.

Nate's hand dipped toward the revolver he wore tied down to his thigh, and the bartender's powerful arms wrapped around him from behind at almost the same instant. Nate's gun hand was pinned before he could touch the grips of his gun.

"Very nice," Longarm said. He raised his glass toward the barkeep.

"I've told you before, Nate, you just gotta quit causing trouble in here or I won't let you back in," the bartender said. "Are you calmed down enough now that I can let you go?"

"These bastards..."

"I heard what you said before," the bartender said patiently. "I heard it last week too. And maybe twice the week before that. I'm gettin' tired of it, Nate Trulock. If you don't quit looking for trouble you're apt to find it sometime, and then where will you be? Why don't you just give it a rest for tonight. Card playin' is bad for you, Nate. Riles your liver something awful. G'wan home now."

The bartender waited for and got a nod from Nate, then released him and started back for his station behind the bar.

Longarm had been chewing on the name the bartender had just used. Nate Trulock. Little Nate Trulock, that was it.

He made the connection from among the hundreds of wanted fliers that routinely came into the Denver offices of the Justice Department. He had no recollection whatsoever about what Little Nate Trulock was wanted for, or where, but he thought it was for something minor.

Still, the little son was standing right there in front of him. And after seeing Trulock's performance with his friends it would be no surprise if his truculence got him in trouble away from home somewhere.

"Nate," Longarm said softly.

"Huh?" Trulock turned and glared at the tall deputy marshal. He looked like a man who needed small provocation to send his constantly simmering anger past the boil-over point. "I don't know you, so shut up or I'll blow a hole through your guts."

"Only if you're good enough," Longarm said. "Though

26

it would be a waste for you to try."

"I just might show you..."

"What you just oughta do, Little Nate, is to take a walk with me and get some legal affairs straightened out."

"What the hell are you bothering me with, mister?"

"There happens to be an outstanding warrant on you. An' I happen to be a deputy United States marshal. That kind of puts you and me in conflict until you tell a judge your side of the story. Once you do that, why, then we can stand up here side by side and have a drink together."

Longarm was speaking gently, wanting to make little of the arrest, hoping Trulock would not insist on letting anger overcome good judgment. But the silly son of a bitch was getting redder and redder above the collar. Longarm set his glass down.

"Listen you, I didn't do nothing over in Nebraska and I ain't gonna be arrested for something I never did," Nate was insisting.

Longarm was no longer listening to his words. He was watching the angry card player's right hand. Behind Nate the card table was suddenly vacated as his recent poker partners ducked out of the line of fire.

"I'd rather you didn't try it, Nate."

"Damn right you would, you chickenshit son of a bitch."

Nate's hand dived for the grips of his revolver, but still Longarm waited, trying to give him a chance to back off at the last split second if only he would.

The effort was wasted, as Longarm had expected it would be. As Nate's gun began to clear leather, Longarm's double-action .44 swept across his belly and lined up square on Nate's chest.

Longarm might have been able to wait a split second longer. But there are limits to patience, and crossing those limits can sometimes have an unhealthy effect. Longarm fired, and Nate was rocked back onto his heels. He still held his revolver in his hand, so Longarm shot him again. Nate's knees were buckling and the second bullet took him in the mouth. It did not do a thing for his looks, and there was going to be quite a mess for someone to clean up when the bar closed.

"Sorry I had to disturb your evening's business," Longarm said to the bartender.

"You tried, I got to give you that. You're really a Federal marshal?"

"Deputy marshal," Longarm corrected. "Would you mind sending somebody to collect Jaybird Nelson?"

"I expect I could do that," the barkeep said. He headed for the other end of the bar to send someone in search of the local deputy. Other men were already bending over Nate Trulock's body.

Longarm took another drink of his rye and hoped Jaybird would not be long in arriving. But what the hell, as a Federal officer Longarm would not be able to collect whatever reward was posted on Trulock. Jaybird might be able to use the money, even if it was no more than fifty dollars.

Longarm shook his head. He wished he could remember what pissant little crime it was that Trulock had been charged with—and that Trulock had died for.

Stupid, Longarm thought. Decidedly stupid. He took another drink of the good Maryland rye and felt much more weary than he had just a few minutes earlier.

## Chapter 4

"Buckskin stud gone wild? Damn right I've heard of him."
The man wiped his hands on a greasy rag, then used the
sleeve of his shirt to wipe sweat out of his eyes. Longarm
had found him in the middle of a repair job on a windmill,
work most stockmen hated since it could not be done from
horseback, but necessary if a man expected to raise his few
head of stock by modern methods. "Come on up t' the house
and I'll tell you what I know about the son of a bitch. I
could use a cup of coffee anyway. And a break from this."
He hooked a thumb toward the windmill that stood above
them, and his tone of voice made it plain that his opinion
of the contraption was not a high one.

Longarm stepped down from his horse and walked beside

29

the rancher, reins trailing behind him and the horse obediently shuffling along. It was late afternoon and the horse had a right to be tired. This was the third ranch Longarm had visited today as he worked his way south.

"Old woman!" the rancher bellowed as they neared the house. "We got a visitor."

The "old woman" came to the door of their soddy to greet her guest, and Longarm automatically swept his Stetson from his head. He knew good and well that the rancher might speak of his wife as his old woman, but if any other man should slight her the score would have to be settled with gunpowder.

"This here fella's lookin' for that buckskin rogue, old woman," the rancher announced. He turned to Longarm. "What'd you say your name was again?"

"Long, ma'am. Deputy United States Marshal Custis Long. Pleasure to meet you, ma'am."

"Marshal, huh? Well, I don't care who they send down here, just so's you get the job done. An' soon. I'm Burl Myers. That there's my old woman. Now come on inside and set."

Longarm accepted the coffee Mrs. Myers poured for him with gratitude, but he wished there was some way he could reasonably refuse the slab of pie that went with it. He was already pied and caked until his insides felt like a sugar loaf from the hospitality of the small ranchers he had been visiting. Still, there was no polite way out, and he smiled as she set the serving—large enough for three growing youngsters—in front of him.

"Mighty nice of you, ma'am," he said. "You were going to tell me about the buckskin?"

"Damn right, I will," Myers said. "Everything I know, including that I want that damn horse shot down wherever he's seen. I'll do it myself if I get the chance to."

"Sounds like you have some reason to want him put down."

"You better believe I do. I got me a nice little place building here. The old woman raises a right fine garden,

30

and I'm not one of these dumb Swedes or such immigrant trash that thinks he can raise a crop on the benefits of wind and dust. No, sir, I ain't. I filed on a quarter-section here an' my old woman filed on another, then we bought a little more as we could afford and leased some besides. I'm small here but lookin' ahead, if you know what I mean."

Longarm nodded and took a bite of the pie. His stomach rebelled, but at least the flavor was decent. Mrs. Myers was a good cook.

"I raise me a few head of heavy draft horses, big old cobs that I'm upgrading by crossing them to a Belgian stud down to Colorado City. And I got thirty-four head of good blooded beeves. They're upgraded too, from the Texas range cattle I started with. Thirty-four head."

"Nice herd," Longarm said agreeably.

"Nice herd, *shit,*" Myers said forcefully. "Until a couple months ago I had thirty-*eight* head. I went out one morning and there was four of my best steers missing. Four of 'em, by damn. And my best."

"You think it was the buckskin rogue that took them, then?"

"I know damn good an' well it was."

"You saw him?" This was a break, Longarm was thinking. So far he had heard about stock losses, but no one had actually seen the buckskin taking them. Myers sounded too positive for that to be the case here. Or so it seemed. Longarm's hopes fell a moment later.

"I didn't see him exactly, but there wasn't no doubt about what done it."

"But if you didn't see him . . ."

"Didn't need to. No need at all. We'd been hearing 'bout him being in the area for a couple of weeks. Couple other fellas lost cattle to him in that time. And I seen his tracks in the draw where my cattle was using. Seen them plain as plain could be. He come drifting in from the south, seen my cattle, and went right into the herd. Cut out the best steers I had and drove them off east somewheres. I tried to follow them, but the ground's so hard an' the grass so dry

31

around here you can't tell a damn thing. Yesterday's tracks don't look hardly no different from last months, and that's when there's any tracks at all, which ain't hardly often. You could pull a steam engine off the rails an' drive it over the prairie around here an' some places I don't think you could get it to more'n make a scratchmark in the ground, it's that dry."

Longarm nodded again. He had already come to the conclusion that if he had to depend on tracking to find the buckskin rogue, the horse was going to have a long and happy life ahead of him.

"How do you know it's the buckskin, though?" Longarm asked.

"Took my best steers, didn't he?"

"That sounds more like a man than a horse."

Myers shook his head and gulped down a slurp of steaming hot coffee. "Not this horse, it don't. That son of a bitch is smarter than most riders. Ask anybody and they'll tell you that much about him. An' I don't just mean since he's gone wild, neither. The buckskin was raised just southwest o' here at the Lazy P. He was another o' the ranch horses there and woulda been gelded and stayed there in the usin' string except that fella Lew Chance bought him as a colt and finished him out as a fancy cutter." Myers shook his head. "Not that he needed much finishing. Just a chance is more like it." He took another deep swallow of the coffee and twisted his neck around to glower at his wife for letting his cup get so low. She refilled it quickly.

"What I was sayin'," he went on, obviously pleased to have an audience willing to listen to him, "is that that horse was a pure natural when it come to cow sense. I seen him myself when he was just a long yearlin', hadn't ever felt a saddle on his back yet nor been taught to do a damn thing. He was running in a holding pasture with a bunch of steers down at the Lazy P. Just a little bunch, it was. But this yearling, he got to playing with them like a pup plays with a soup bone. He'd gather them into a bunch and move them into this corner, and then he'd go find himself a patch of

32

shade and crop some grass. But you could see he was keeping an eye on them cows too. They'd start to spread out a bit looking for a mouthful of grass, and here'd come that colt. He'd gather them up again an' move them into another corner. Then he'd go back to his shade. Every time them cows scattered, he'd be on 'em again. Move them here, move them there. It was something to watch, an' I said at the time, I told old Charlie Rawls that that right there was a colt to watch because he was going to be a helluva cuttin' hoss. You can ask old Charlie. He'll remember it too. He's still over at the Lazy P, matter of fact. He'll remember."

Longarm nodded. He had his suspicions about Myers's foresight as it was seen now in hindsight, but the man sounded like he was telling a story that he believed. And Longarm himself had seen one or two yearlings that possessed that degree of instinct for herding. It was rare but not unheard of.

"Later on, well, I expect you've heard the stories already about how good that horse was."

"I surely have. He must have been something to watch."

"I should hope to go belly up if it ain't the truth," Myers said firmly. He looked around. "Something to watch nowadays too, maybe. The horse is plumb crazy, as I expect you've also heard."

"I don't know what you mean."

Myers gave his wife a look of sudden annoyance. "Get out and tend your garden a while, old woman."

Obediently Mrs. Myers—she was probably in her middle twenties, Longarm guessed, and might well have been her much older husband's second or even third wife—refilled both men's coffee cups, then gathered her skirts and hurried outside into the blinding glare of the afternoon heat.

"You ain't heard that the horse has turned, well, peculiar?" Myers asked.

"No, I don't believe I have, beyond the obvious things—that he's stealing cattle and maybe has killed men."

"Hell, that's just the half of it. You know, of course, that he's a stud horse. Never cut."

33

"Yeah?"

"Well, what they say is that this damn fool stallion is so crazy from all the beatings he took or whatever that he's taken to mounting cows instead o' mares. He don't know what he is any more."

"That sounds a bit incredible, don't you think?"

"Maybe you say so, but I'll tell you what. The time he come around here stealing my cattle, I had a pair of mares out near them, and one o' my mares was in season. She was so hot my neighbor'd had to pen his stud horse lest I sue him for damages by lettin' his scrungy stud pony get to my good mare. An' if that old buckskin had him the sense that a normal horse does, there wouldn't of been any way to keep him off my mare short of a bullet. But there wasn't a hint of anything like that, and the mare come around regular as could be the next month when I carried her down to the Belgian stud. Now if *that* don't prove it, I don't know what would."

Longarm grunted politely, but his own opinion was that the only thing proven was that Burl Myers was carrying a short load between his ears.

Oh, he could believe that a stallion might lack interest in a mare. Those were no more rare than truly excellent cow horses.

But one that would mate with a *cow?*

That one Longarm was going to have to observe personally before he believed it, and even then he would admire any man who would be able to train a horse to a trick like that. Frankly, Longarm did not believe it could be done. He resolved to take stories about the buckskin rogue with several extra grains of salt in the future.

It probably also would be a good idea to find the Lazy P and talk to some of the boys there who should have known the horse, he decided.

At least he had gotten that much benefit from his conversation with Burl Myers. That and a piece of pie.

Longarm sighed and began to shovel the pie into his mouth in earnest. He had a suspicion that if he did not finish it Myers would take it as a sign of disapproval with his "old woman" and her cooking. Longarm could get along very nicely after he left without having to wonder if Mrs. Myers was taking a pounding because Deputy Marshal Custis Long was too full to eat the poor woman's pie.

"I thank you for your help," he said as he finished. He stood and tried to hide a belch that wanted to erupt past his sweeping mustache.

"You ain't leavin', are you? Why, I got lots more to tell."

"Thanks, Mr. Myers, but I have to get on about my duties, much as I'd enjoy staying." There were some lies that were excusable, Longarm figured.

It was well after dark before he reached the town—it was really more of a settlement than a town, with only a handful of businesses and houses to mark its place against the foot of the Front Range mountains—and he was more than ready for a meal and a bed.

Somehow he had managed to miss the Lazy P. And he was not about to turn around and go looking for it now. He pulled his horse to a stop in front of the first place he came to with lights showing and tied the animal to the hitch rail there.

"Just exactly what I was needing," he said when he got inside. He had blundered into a greasy spoon restaurant that was as welcome to him now as the Brown Palace would have been.

"Did you say something, sir?"

"What . . . oh, I didn't see you there." Longarm removed his hat politely.

The gesture was not hard to make. The girl, waitress or possibly even proprietress, was the nicest thing he had seen all day long. She had been standing beside the door with a cloth in her hands and must have been engaged in cleaning the tables. The evening's dinner trade obviously had already been and gone because most of the tables, although now empty, showed signs of recent use.

35

Longarm smiled and took a second look. Damned if the girl did not look even better that time.

Tall and slender, she wore her hair loose in a golden flow that spilled down her back nearly to her waist. Her eyes were a pale, almost gray blue set in a face with high cheekbones and full lips. She wore a checked gingham dress and full-length white apron, but the garments were unable to hide a mouthful-sized swell of breast and a trimly swelling haunch with a handspan waist in between.

She began to look nervous and took half a step backward. Longarm quickly took his eyes from her and nodded toward the empty tables. "You're still serving, I hope."

"Yes, sir."

He chose a clean table against the wall and made himself comfortable, trying with limited success to keep from staring at the pretty girl, who now came over to take his order.

"I'd like..."

"We don't have that."

"What?"

She gave him a grudging smile. "I wasn't trying to be rude. It's just that no matter what you might want, we are out of everything except pork chops and baked beans. Will that do?"

"Reckon it will have to," he said. She started to turn away. "Miss?"

"Yes, sir?"

"A moment ago you looked a bit frightened. I apologize. I am Deputy United States Marshal Custis Long. If I did anything to offend you, feel free to report me to my superiors. I'd be glad to tell you where you could find my boss."

"Oh." She drew a deep sigh of relief. "Thank goodness."

"That you can report me?"

She shook her head, and Longarm was unable to keep himself from noticing what the movement did to the way her hair shimmered in the lamplight.

"You aren't who I thought you might be."

Again she would have turned away, but Longarm pushed

36

a chair out and motioned for her to sit with him.

"That sounds like something specific," he said. "Besides, you don't look like a particularly flighty girl. Very pretty, but not silly about it." He smiled. "I'm a pretty fair hand as a listener."

"Oh, I wouldn't want to bother you with it."

"No bother." He pulled out a cheroot and match and made himself comfortable in the chair. He wanted her to get the message that he was willing to sit and listen for as long as she cared to speak.

"If you're sure?" she asked hesitantly.

"Go ahead."

"It isn't anything that would interest a United States marshal, really."

"Deputy. And I am interested. Personally if not professionally."

"All right, then, but really it's just a drab little story. There is . . . a man. . . ."

Longarm nodded. Pretty as this girl was, he could believe there would be lots of them.

"I saw this gentleman—well—socially . . . once. Now I don't want to see him again. And he does not want to take no for an answer. He threatened to have me brought to him by force if necessary. And I was afraid for a moment that you might be . . ."

"I understand. Look, everybody has the right to change his mind. Or hers. I'll tell you what, I'll make a deal with you."

She began to look suspicious again.

"No, nothing like that. You tell me where I can find the best hotel or boarding house in town, and I'll walk you home safely when you're done here. Is that fair?"

She looked relieved. "That is quite fair."

She brought his meal, and he ate quickly. He smoked contentedly while the girl finished cleaning up, and she locked the door behind them as he accompanied her outside.

Longarm draped the reins of his horse over one arm and offered the other to the girl.

They had not taken three steps when a man detached himself from the shadows and stepped into their path.

"Giving it to strangers now?" he growled. He was ignoring Longarm and stood menacingly over the slender girl.

"Excuse me," Longarm said politely. "Are you the gentleman in question or a hired hand?"

"What the fuck do you care?" the man demanded.

"It does make a difference, actually." Longarm was smiling, and the fellow seemed not to have noticed the sudden hardness in the gunmetal blue of Longarm's eyes.

"I got a prior claim to this ore, if that's what you want to know."

"As a joke that didn't do much for me," Longarm said. He looked at the girl. "Is this the gentleman you could do without?"

She nodded. She looked too frightened to speak.

"Thank you."

The man was as tall as Longarm and much more heavily built. He seemed used to the idea that his size and perhaps his reputation would intimidate anyone he came across, but intimidation was not one of Longarm's weaknesses.

The man raised a clubbed fist over Longarm's smiling face and did his best to look nasty and mean. In return he suddenly could feel a small steel ring pressed against the underside of his chin. He had not seen Longarm's hand move and had no idea where the Colt came from.

He swallowed. Hard.

"Shall we step around the side of the building here? It will only take a moment." Still smiling, Longarm turned back to the girl. "I'll be right back."

She nodded, a look of blank shock on her face.

Longarm and the disruptive gentleman disappeared from her view, and as Longarm had promised he was back in little more than seconds.

"Did you . . . ?"

"Oh, he's fine. I don't think he'll bother you again, though. I introduced myself. We discussed your preferences. If he does bother you again, which I doubt, just let me know."

The girl sagged against him with relief, and Longarm was uncomfortably aware of the warmth that came from her trim body. She began to cry.

"Hey, it's all right now, miss. I'll walk you home, and you'll be safe as safe can be. But you have to keep your end of the bargain. You have to show me to a good room for the night."

Her sniffling slowed, and she wiped her teary eyes against the front of Longarm's vest.

"I wish I knew how I could thank you." She looked up at him. And there was probably no way she could have avoided feeling the reaction he was having to the way she was pressed against his body. The tears stopped and she began to smile. "Well, maybe I do know a way at that."

"Yes?"

"There really is no decent hotel or boarding house here."

"Um?"

"And I do have a rather large bed in my room, you see." She was playing with his collar now and tickling the chest hairs that showed at his throat.

"Your friend might come back tonight after all," Longarm suggested.

"I would worry about that. I really would."

He smiled and put an arm around her narrow waist. "I wouldn't want you to worry about anything."

He trailed the pretty girl to her room and waited patiently while she used a sulphur match to light the single lamp in the room. Her hair caught the lamplight with a glow of soft gold on even softer, finer gold, and she turned to him with a smile traced on her lips.

The girl melted into Longarm's embrace, and the taste of her was sweet. Her breath tasted good in his mouth, and there was a yielding softness in that slender body that aroused him.

He was puzzled for a moment when she pulled abruptly

39

away. He was sure he had not misinterpreted the rapidity of her breathing. But still, as he had already told her, a person has the right to a change of mind.

She cocked her head and smiled. And began to undress.

There was no coyness about her, nothing of the tease. She shed her clothes quickly and once again pressed herself to him. Her breathing was coming very rapidly now.

Longarm kissed her, then shifted slightly and bent to trace the curve of her neck and shoulders with his lips. The girl moaned began to press her pelvis back and forth.

Her breasts were small but firm and exquisitely formed. He pulled a hard rosebud of nipple into his mouth and teased her with the flick of his tongue.

"Please. Now," she breathed. She was fumbling with his belt and trouser buttons.

Still clutching each other, they found the bed, and Longarm bent over her. He was clothed except for his trousers and balbriggans sagging to his boot tops, but that did not seem to bother her at all.

The girl was moistly ready for him, and she drew him into herself at once, sighing at the filling contact.

Longarm was prepared to take his time, to make their joining last as long as possible, but she was not. Demandingly, she pumped against his belly, slapping the softness of her flesh against him with an urgency that was rare.

Within moments, within strokes, Longarm felt her stiffen beneath him and felt the warm explosion of her breath against his neck.

Still embedded within her body, he raised up slightly to look at her. "You couldn't possibly have..."

She smiled. "I did." She said it with no small amount of satisfaction. She sighed. "Now, if you are ready to continue, so am I."

Longarm grinned at her. "I expect I could do that."

Several hours later Longarm yawned and lolled his head on the single pillow they were sharing. "Could I ask you a question? A rather personal question?"

"Of course. Anything."

Come to think of it, he decided, she did not have much to hide from him at this point. Couldn't have.

"Would you mind telling me your name?"

She laughed and nuzzled against the base of his neck. Which led to other nuzzlings and explorations, and soon neither of them was laughing.

But it was morning and Longarm was miles away before he realized that the darn girl never *had* told him her name.

# Chapter 5

Longarm rode deep in thought. There were more than enough things he still had to check out in this investigation, but none of them seemed particularly promising. If anything, they made him feel slightly foolish. The idea of sending a deputy United States marshal out to do battle with a runaway cutting horse was ridiculous.

And so far, chasing a horse seemed to be just about all he was accomplishing. His investigation had produced no nibbles to the bait that was being temptingly spread for whoever it was who had murdered Charles Wolfe and the other hunter who had preceded him. As a murder investigation this whole thing seemed to be turning into a nice ride in the country.

He shrugged his shoulders and rode on. Billy had thrown him out onto the plains as bait, and bait he would continue to be.

He stopped at another ranch, heard more stories about the alleged prowess of the buckskin rogue—which Longarm was privately coming to believe was either a ghost or the smartest damn horse ever foaled—and, more important, got better directions to the Lazy P. He finally found the correct set of headquarters buildings shortly before noon.

"Mornin'," he said to a pair of loafers by the bunkhouse door when he rode in. Apparently the place was not so huge nor the work so far-flung that the hands could not come in for their dinner here. He sat on his horse waiting for an invitation to step down and join them.

The two cowhands took their time looking him over, and the older of the two pulled a pipe from his coat pocket and fussed over its proper loading and lighting while he pretended to ignore Longarm. Finally he spoke.

"You don't look like you're after work. Not dressed so pretty, you don't. Don't look hungry enough to be ridin' the grubline neither."

"I don't expect you'll ever find out if I have to turn and ride off from here," Longarm told him.

"True enough." The hand—he was sun-weathered and wrinkled enough to be in his late fifties at least—pulled on his pipe, examined it for a moment, and added, "Reckon you could light an' set for a while, then. Dinner'll be ready directly, and the boss here is a sociable fella. Sez we shouldn't turn away strays even if they're fixed up like dudes."

"Nice of him," Longarm said. He got down and led the horse to the nearest hitch rail.

"Don't see many o' them McClellan saddles," the old cowhand observed.

"Comfortable," Longarm said. He loosened his cinch to let the horse blow and went to join the Lazy P hands in their front-door loafing.

The younger one still had not spoken nor barely done more than acknowledge that Longarm existed. The older one squinted at Longarm's vest and asked, "Denver?"

Longarm nodded. "How'd you know?" He pulled a cheroot from his pocket and busied himself with lighting it.

"The stitching. Homer Garcia made me a pair o' chaps a while back. That looks like his work."

"It is," Longarm agreed. He took another look at the old fellow. The cowhand looked like any drawling hayseed with the seat of his jeans worn shiny from time in the saddle. Often enough such aging cowhands were no brighter than their simple, pastoral occupations might imply. Yet there were others who lived and worked in the outdoors who developed an almost uncanny level of observation and had the mental abilities to match. It seemed that this observant old-timer might be one of that latter category.

"City fella?" the old-timer asked.

"Sometimes," Longarm said. The old cowhand looked at his loafing partner but made no comment. "I'm a deputy United States marshal," Longarm added. "Custis Long."

The old cowhand grunted and chewed on the stem of his pipe. Longarm felt vaguely uncomfortable. He felt sure that the old boy was thinking that he was a political appointee gorging at the public trough instead of a capable peace officer. Longarm was convinced of it when the oldtimer took another long look at his vest. It was a rare feeling and one Longarm did not like, but damned if he was going to offer any explanations to this old man.

"They call me Handy," the old fellow said after too many moments had slipped past.

"Because you are?"

"Something like that." He nodded. "This talkative jasper on my right is John Paul Patterson. We call him Jyp." Jyp still had not spoken but now at least he nodded.

Longarm took a long pull on his cheroot and wondered why in hell he should care what Handy thought anyway. He could not answer himself. There was just something about the old fellow that said he more than lived up to his name.

"Dinner time," Handy said, although there had been no

bell or triangle rung to announce it. Handy and Jyp stood up and began walking toward the ranch house, and Longarm joined them. They were nearly there before Longarm saw a small knot of mounted hands arriving. They had ridden in from behind the house, and Handy must have heard them coming before Longarm was aware of them. Longarm's estimation of the old boy rose another notch.

The Lazy P hands crowded into the long chow hall that was part of the ranch house, and Longarm found himself introduced to a foreman named Tod Brent and to half a dozen other men whose names he did not catch. Without being obvious about it, he finagled his way to a seat between Handy and the foreman Brent.

Handy had lagged behind the others when they took their places and grabbed their plates, but now he personally appeared at Longarm's side with a heavy crockery plate in his hand extended toward the deputy marshal.

"Here y' go, Custis," he said.

"Thanks." Longarm reached around to the other side of the plate and took it by the same edge Handy was holding. He smiled politely and set the plate on the table, brushing his fingertips across the nearer edge as he withdrew his hand. As he had more than half expected, the heavy plate had been resting on the side of a hot stove and the one edge was burning hot, though the part Handy had been holding was only pleasantly warm.

It was a common enough trick to apply to visiting dudes. When the dude took hold of the fiercely hot china he would naturally complete his examination in a hurry. The normal result was a dropped and broken plate and deep embarrassment for the uninitiated guest. Longarm had dropped a plate in his time, but that had been a long time ago, and not where old Handy could see it happen. He was not going to be caught by the same trick twice.

Neither Longarm nor Handy gave any hint of expression to indicate Longarm's escape of the joke.

They sat, and the table full of men began loading their plates with heaping mounds of starchy foods and fried meats.

At least, Longarm thought, a ranch cook knows how a man likes to eat.

"U. S. marshal, huh?" Brent asked when they were nearly finished with the hurriedly consumed meal.

"Deputy," Longarm corrected.

"Here on official business?"

"Sort of. Horse hunting."

"Horse hunting?" Brent asked. A number of eyebrows were raised around the table. "Handy there used to do quite a bit of horse hunting himself. Over Utah way, wasn't it, Handy?"

"Ayuh. There an' the Western Slope region." He looked at Longarm and leaned closer. "I don't know if you're familiar with the area, Custis, but I mind one time I was after a bunch of wild ones over southwest of Brown's Hole."

Longarm nodded and pulled a cigar from his pocket. Some of the other men were lighting up, too.

"Horses then was going for five dollars a head straight off the range or fifteen dollars broke out. But there was this Mormon—had him more wives than a sensible man would want to have to listen to all at one time—who had a hankering for one particular stallion. Color of a new-minted double eagle, this horse was, and he throwed his color true. Nearly every colt in his band o' mares had yella coats the match of their pappy's, and this old Mormon wanted to get the stud so's he could breed him to a bunch of good mares and get a bunch of matched saddle an' driving horses for all his wives. Wanted them all alike so's nobody would get jealous, I reckon." He pulled his pipe out and began loading it. "I can see how that could get to be a problem." He finished the chore and lighted up.

"The old boy told me he'd pay a hundred dollars for that yella horse an' I wouldn't even have to break him. Sounded like pretty good money at the time."

Longarm nodded again and sat back in his chair. The other hands looked mighty interested in Handy's story.

"Real dry, broken country over that way, an' not too many places a bunch of horses could water, so I figured it

46

should be no trick to find out where they was using and trap them when they come in to drink. Spent a couple weeks studying the tracks of this particular bunch and finally worked out that they watered every third day at a seep way back in a box canyon under this flat-top mesa. Regular as a clock, they were. Maybe more so.

"The days they was off somewhere else I'd work on a fence across the mouth o' that canyon. You know, covering it over with brush and whatnot so they couldn't see it was a fence, and adding to it a bit at a time so they wouldn't realize they was being closed down to a narrower and narrower gap all the time.

"I had my outfit parked up on the rim, and I thought I was pretty well set, but I kept noticing that I had less an' less supplies than I'd thought. Thought I'd packed in enough to last me a couple months, but after just a little time I seen I was running out of bacon and my fresh beef was et up almost before I knowed it, and pretty soon I was down to nothing but flour and salt and such dry stuff as don't do much for a man's belly. That and a few canned things, and half of them didn't have the labels on so I couldn't tell what I did have.

"Still, I was close to putting that hundred dollars in my pocket, so I figured I could hang out as long as it took, which I figured would not be much longer."

Handy rambled on and on in a dull, dry voice, describing his camp layout and every twist and crevice of the canyon floor and a dozen or more small caves within the canyon. Longarm found his eyes growing heavy from the combined effects of the meal and the drone of Handy's voice.

"So I pulled the gate across the mouth of my fence," the old hand was saying, "an' rode up there thinkin' to rope the yella stud and turn the mares loose once I had the one I wanted."

Longarm yawned.

"It was coming dusk by then, but o' course them wild horses don't come to water hardly except in the dark and there was no help for that.

47

"I rode up into that canyon in the little light that was left, an' I come up alongside this cave down below the seep—I told you about that cave, didn't I?—an' sure enough there I seen this bright yella animal heading for the water in the almost night.

"I built a big old Blocker loop since the light was so poor an' I put the spurs to my pony. The son of a bitch didn't like it. He squealed and bawled some, but he was a stout old thing and a roping horse that wouldn't quit. I spurred him the second time and he took off after that yella thing just ahead of us.

"The yella didn't run as fast as I'd expected, and I was on him in a minute. Got that Blocker loop to rolling and let 'er fly. Took him with as good a head catch as I've ever made in my life, snatched the slack fast as you've got to go with a big loop like that, whipped on my dallies, and went to fighting.

"Damnedest roaring I ever heard filled that there canyon. The yella plumb turned on me and charged my horse with his jaws snapping and the slobber flying." He shook his head sadly. "It was fearsome, I tell you." Handy sighed and reached for his coffee cup. He acted for all the world as if he had totally lost interest in the rest of his story.

"So what happened?" Longarm asked the obligatory question.

Handy looked up at him. "What? Oh. Turned out it weren't the yella horse I roped after all. It was a damned old yella grizzly bear. The same one that had been eating my meat and stuff." Again he stopped and went back to his coffee.

"Well?" Longarm demanded.

"The grizzly? Ah, I just roped him down and sold *him* to the Mormon. Never did see that yella stud horse again."

"Just so you came out all right," Longarm drawled. He crushed out the remains of his cheroot in a dirty plate and let his head loll back. "You know, Handy, that reminds me of a time a few years ago when I was helping a friend do some roping down in the Arizona country." He launched into his own story, making it up as he went along, the only thing certain about it being that it should top Handy's.

Much later, the afternoon's work quite thoroughly interrupted, the men moved out onto the wide porch hung onto the side of the ranch house, and Longarm came to the point of his visit.

"It's no big secret," he said, "that what the Justice Department has asked me to do down here is help out Interior by getting rid of a buckskin cutting horse that's turned rogue. I'm told the horse came off this spread."

"Old Buck?" Brent asked. "Hell, we most all of us know that horse. Or did." He hooked a thumb toward the senior hand of the outfit. "Handy there prob'ly knows him better than anyone."

Handy nodded. "He's a horse, all right. Some animal, that Buck, and I'm not funning you a bit there. That crazy Lew Chance bought him, and I was almost glad he did. Removed the temptation I was having my own self."

Longarm gave him an inquiring look.

"Yeah, me. You might know, son, that an old fossil like me has no business playing nursemaid to a damned stud horse, but Buck was so good he was tempting me, and that's a fact. It's been years since I owned any kind of a horse, but I sure came close to it with him. Might have done it if Lew hadn't put up his money first. Hell, I broke that horse out when he was a colt."

"Did most of the cutting training on him too, if the truth be known," Brent added.

"Aw," Handy said with a wave of his hand. "That there Buck was so smart he didn't hardly need any training. It was just naturally in him to work cows. Couldn't hardly have kept him from doing it if I'd tried."

"Still can't," another Lazy P hand said over his shoulder. "At least the way I hear it."

Longarm looked at the man, and he seemed familiar. It took only a moment to make the proper connection. The hand was wearing a mustache now, but take that away and give him a different hat and he was one of the three hands in the photograph Billy Vail had given Longarm back in Denver.

Longarm pulled the picture out and showed it around.

"Sure," the fellow said, "I remember when we had this taken. A couple years it's been now. That's Lew there." He pointed. "And this is Tom Morris. And o' course that's me. We used to pal around a lot."

"You all know the horse then," Longarm said.

"Know him? We used to. Nowadays we just hear about him."

"Lose any stock to him?" Longarm asked.

Brent shook his head. "Not that we know of. Of course, we run more head than most of the folks around here. And a lot of our business is raising horses too. Old Buck's only interested in cattle. Besides, he'd have memories of that damn fool Lew around here. Hating Lew and those beatings is what set him off to start with. I expect he doesn't want to come back here because he was beaten a lot in the corrals over yonder."

Longarm nodded. It was a sensible enough conclusion. A horse is not particularly smart, but it has a memory better than an elephant's highly reputed recall. If a horse boogers at ghosts and goblins beside a rock in a trail he travels once, the odds are he will remember it and booger again the next time he passes that same rock, even if the interval between trips is a month or more. And no creature wants to take a beating.

"None of you has seen him then?" Longarm asked. He looked around the ring of Lazy P hands and got only head-shakes for answers.

"Have you heard about anything he's done around here recently?" Longarm asked.

"Nothing since Morales was killed. That's about a week past," the foreman said.

"Morales?" The name was a new one to Longarm. He had heard that the buckskin was supposed to be a killer, but this was the first name since Lew Chance.

"Mexican fella," Brent explained. "He had a place south

50

of here. Buck killed him beside his windmill, the way I heard it."

"Could you give me directions to the place?" Longarm asked. He had intended to go looking for the woman the Elbert County deputy had heard about who was supposed to have seen the horse, but this sounded more promising.

He thanked Brent for the meal and reclaimed his horse from the hitch rail. Handy had trailed along beside him and spoke as Longarm tightened his cinch.

"If I can help you, Marshal—well, I know old Buck better than anybody." He smiled. "An', hell, you ain't as bad a sort as I thought."

"For a city fellow?"

Handy grinned. "Exactly."

Longarm settled his hat and swung onto his horse. It was going to be a long ride to the Morales place and he probably would not make it before nightfall.

"I'll keep that in mind, Handy. Thanks." He bumped the horse into a road-eating jog and set out toward the south.

# Chapter 6

The camp was not bad for a dry stop. He built his fire in the lee of one of those tilted slabs of red rock that cropped out above the surface of the soil here and there on the plains along the Front Range. The outcropping was perhaps fifty feet long and fifteen high and made an excellent windbreak. A jumble of broken rock down the slight incline from the slab acted as a reflector for the heat from his fire. The days were warm now but the nights were chilly, and the wind carried a bite in it once the sun slipped below the mountains so clearly visible to the west. From where he sat, Longarm could see the southwestward swing of the mountain range that led to the deep indentation that was the Arkansas Valley and, north along the Front Range, the faint but clearly visible notch that was Ute Pass.

Longarm probably could have found a ranch house to spend the night in if he had ridden farther, but the benefits would not have been worth the effort. And he enjoyed his own company well enough that he did not mind a night alone with nothing but the sound of the wind and of his horse cropping dried grass stems to keep him company. He ate a sparse meal from the supplies he carried in his saddlebags, held out enough water from his canteen to make coffee, and gave the remainder to the horse. Come morning he would have to find a place to get water for the animal and for himself, but the country was too densely settled for him to have to regard that as a problem. And for the moment he was content.

He leaned back against the polished seat of his ball-buster McClellan saddle, comfortable more from long use than from design but remarkably easy on a horse's back, and reached for a cheroot.

The borrowed horse, its silhouette visible against the slightly paler black of the star-studded night sky, raised its head to stare off into the darkness. It stopped chewing and its ears twitched forward.

Longarm sat up and his hand automatically dropped into his lap. His fingertips reassured him that the double-action Colt .44 was in place in front of his left hip.

The horse had given him the first warning, but he could hear it too now, the rhythmic fall of shod hooves nearing his camp. There was more than one horse coming in, but he could not be sure beyond that.

"Howdy," a voice called when the riders were still out of sight.

"Come on in."

There were two of them. Longarm could see their horses in the fringes of the firelight, but he could not make out their brands.

"We saw your fire. Hope you don't mind company, because I think you've found the best spot for a couple miles around," one of them said.

He stepped into the circle of light, a young, rosy-cheeked

cowboy with blond hair showing under his hat and a smile that displayed dazzling white teeth. He looked like a kid any mother would want her daughter to marry: young and fresh and cheerfully good-natured.

His partner was considerably older, in his mid-thirties at least. He had hair as black as an Indian's and nearly as greasy, and his face showed the stubble of several days of going without a shave.

As was to be expected, both carried revolvers stuffed into the large pouches—almost leather sacks—that served most men as holsters. Both men wore well-used chaps—wind-cheaters more than brush-busters in this part of the country—and spurs with small rowels, unlike the Mexican cartwheel rowels favored further south.

"You're welcome to light," Longarm said, "but I've used the last of my water."

"No problem, we have enough," the younger of them said. "And we thank you."

Longarm nodded.

The two unsaddled and hobbled their horses before turning them loose to graze. The older one produced a coffee pot and a canteen and put the pot on the fire, while the younger spread bedrolls for both of them.

"I'm Bob," the handsome youngster said, "and this is my big brother Lee." He was as smiling and likeable as a snake-oil salesman.

"I'm Custis Long, boys."

"Marshal Long?" Lee, the older brother, was not smiling.

"Deputy," Longarm agreed. "How'd you know that?"

"We heard you were down here chasing a horse or something. Heard you got into a scrap up in Castle Rock, too. Word like that gets around some."

"So it does." Longarm yawned and reached for a cheroot.

"What was it happened up in Castle Rock?" Lee asked.

Longarm pulled up a few stems of grass, ignited them in the fire, and used them to light his smoke. He shrugged. "Fella got nervous about the thought of jail, I reckon. Pity of it was that he wasn't wanted for anything very important.

54

But there was paper out on him and I had to take him in. It wasn't important."

Lee nodded and squatted over the coffee pot to shake a cloth-wrapped wad of once-used grounds into the pot. Bob was still smiling.

"Is that cayuse over there yours?" Lee asked.

"Borrowed," Longarm said. "He belongs to a man over in Fountain now, but I won't deliver him until I'm done with him."

"Looks like a decent animal. Covers ground pretty good, does he?" Lee went on.

"Not bad. Why?"

"Oh, I'm just notional," Lee said. "I see a horse and sometimes I want him. Mind showing him to me?"

"There wouldn't be any point in it," Longarm said. "I already told you, he isn't mine to sell."

"Yeah, well, I wouldn't mind looking him over while the coffee's brewing. I might buy him off the new owner if I like him. Come on." Lee stood up and gestured for Longarm to join him.

It was a foolish request, Longarm felt, and a waste of time. On the other hand, it would be just as pointless to argue with Lee, even if Lee's worn clothing and unlikely appearance made Longarm doubt that the man could afford much of a price for that or any other horse. Longarm stood and turned to follow Lee away from the fire.

Behind him Longarm heard the oily, metallic *cla-clack* that comes only from the sound of a single-action hammer being drawn past half-cock into firing position. "Son of a bitch," he muttered.

He turned. Bob was standing with a revolver leveled at Longarm's gut. The gun was an ancient Colt .36 Navy cap and ball revolver that some gunsmith had converted to fire the more modern .38 rimfire cartridge. The .38 was underpowered for any serious work. But it could still blow one hell of a hole through a man, and the range was close. The handsome, likeable, trustworthy-looking youngster was still smiling.

"You boys are not shy about who you steal horses from, are you?" Longarm said.

"Oh, we didn't come here to steal no horse from you, Marshal. No, sir, we wouldn't do a thing like that." Bob's smile became almost cherubic. "That wouldn't be honest."

"You wouldn't mind if I asked what you're up to then, would you?"

"In a minute." Bob moved a step closer. They were almost belly to belly now, and it would have been difficult for even an excited halfwit to miss a man-sized target at that range. Longarm had seen it happen before, but he was not going to stake his life on a repeat performance. And Bob did not look particularly excited or nervous at the moment. The youngster nodded and Longarm felt Lee moving up beside him.

The older brother snaked Longarm's .44 from its holster and bent to retrieve the .44-40 Winchester from beside Longarm's saddle as well.

"Reckon his claws are pulled now, Bobby."

Bob grinned. "Thanks, big brother." He motioned with the barrel of his revolver for Longarm to resume his seat. "Coffee will be ready directly, Marshal."

Longarm sat. "You're awful polite for a highwayman. Assuming that's what you are up to. I notice you haven't said yet." He finished his cheroot and ground it out in the hard-baked earth at his side.

Bob sat crosslegged on the ground a few yards to Longarm's right. The muzzle of the old Colt never wavered.

"That shooting that you don't figure as important, Marshal," Lee said. "We think it was plenty important."

"That was our brother," Bob added.

"He was feisty, but he wasn't a bad kid."

"Never meant no real harm to nobody."

"But you wouldn't take that for an answer. You had to go an' shoot him down like he was some kind of criminal."

"I told you," Longarm said. "There was paper out on him. It's for a judge to decide if he was guilty of anything, not me. But when he drew on me he didn't give me any

56

choice but to take him the hard way." He looked from one to the other of them, looking them square in the eyes. "If you want me to apologize for doing my job, or for living through it, I'm afraid I have to disappoint you. I did what I had to do. I'd do it exactly the same way again."

"Oh, we give you credit for that much, Marshal," Bob said. Damned if the kid didn't *still* look likeable and innocent. "But we got to do what's right by our kin. I hope you can understand that."

"So what is it that you figure is right by your kin?"

"It's simple, Marshal," Lee said. "Maybe you've read the book we got it from? It's an eye for an eye, a tooth for a tooth."

"It's pretty plain, Marshal," young Bob said with a smile.

"Funny," Longarm said. "I've read the same book all right, but somehow I got a different message out of it. Mind if I smoke?" He smiled. "I've been trying to cut down, but somehow I don't think this is a good time for it."

"Go ahead."

He fingered another cheroot out of his vest pocket, found a match, and flicked it alight with his thumbnail. "Coffee's starting to boil," he said. Lee moved to the fire and bent to get the pot.

Longarm shook his head. "I'd always thought I'd die in bed, some time just before dawn, the way most old folks seem to slip away." He slipped his fingers into the watch pocket of his vest. "You're absolutely sure about this, are you?"

"We're sure," Bob said with another brilliant smile.

Longarm nodded.

The little .44 derringer hooked onto the end of Longarm's watch chain in place of a fob snapped and spat fire into the night. A third socket appeared in young Bob's forehead like a spare eye, but this one was blank and oozing dark blood.

The boy's body slumped backward onto the hard soil with his old Colt cold and unfired.

"Don't," Longarm warned quickly.

Lee had dropped the coffee pot into the fire, nearly extinguishing the small flame. He stood staring at his dead brother, his face screwed into a mask of anguish.

"Don't try it," Longarm warned again. The derringer was aimed at Lee's belly, and if the range of several yards was long for such a weapon it was still close enough.

"That's two you got to answer for!" Lee cried.

Longarm had no time to explain or reason. Lee straightened and tried to fumble his revolver out of his crude holster.

It was an extraordinarily stupid thing for a grown man to do, but Longarm had no choice now. And with only the inaccurate derringer in his hand, he could afford to take no chances.

The little gun spat its second and final bullet, and Lee doubled over as if he had just been punched in the gut. He coughed and sat down.

Longarm was on his feet before Lee hit the ground. He leaped to Lee's side and plucked the revolver, another Civil War reject that had been converted to cartridge use, from the man's holster. Longarm threw it aside and retrieved his own weapons before he reloaded the little .44 and put it away.

"I wish you hadn't done that," he said. He meant it.

"No choice, Marshal. You read the book."

"I also read the law, damn it," Longarm said.

"We did what we had to do," Lee said. He was hunched over, holding himself and moaning. Longarm guessed that the fierce pain of the low belly wound was beginning to reach him.

"Am I dying?" Lee asked.

"I don't know." Longarm laid the man back and fumbled to open the buttons on his shirt and trousers. The wound was a barely visible puncture an inch below and two inches to the right of Lee's navel. Only a few drops of blood were collected on the surface, but it was impossible to know what damage might have been done inside.

Longarm shook his head. "I just can't tell. I've seen men get up and walk away within a week of getting a wound like that."

Lee grimaced. "And I've seen 'em die screaming like

schoolgirls in an hour or a day." He winced. "Bobby and Nate, they was too young to go off to the War, but I wasn't. I seen things then that no man ever oughta see."

He groped blindly with his hand and Longarm clasped it. He had shot the man, but he held no malice for him.

"I hope . . ." Longarm began, but Lee cut him off with an almost violent shake of his head.

"No," he said. "Jail's not for me, no more'n it would have been for poor Nate. I'd rather end it here. Could I ask you a favor?"

"You can ask."

"If I get like some boys I've seen—if I start bellering and making a fuss—would you mind helping me the last little way over?" He gave Longarm a look that was half grimace and half smile, and for the first time Longarm could see a faint resemblance between the dark Lee and the blond, boyish, smiling Bobby. "I'm looking forward to crossing over anyway, you understand. It wouldn't be a thing you'd have to feel bad about."

"I would help you if I could," Longarm said, "but you're asking for a thing I cannot do. I'm truly sorry, but I couldn't."

Lee nodded. "I was afraid of that." His frame shuddered and went rigid as a wave of pain hit him, arcing his body completely off the ground for a moment. The color drained from his face and beads of sweat popped out on his forehead. He relaxed. "Sure wish you'd change your mind. I think it's going to be bad."

"I wish I could help."

"I know. I ain't blaming you."

He was quiet for a time. "Marshal?"

"Yes."

"Our name. On the marker. Would you see that it's spelled right?"

"Of course."

Lee Trulock had him spell it to make sure it would be right. "And a cross or some nice little saying?" he went on.

"Sure. Is, uh, is there any family I should notify? Anyone I should ship you to?"

Lee shook his head. "I'm the last one now. You won't

59

be having to look over your shoulder for more of us, if that's what you've been thinking."

"No, Lee, that wasn't what I was wondering about."

"I guess maybe you wouldn't be at that."

He began to cough, and each heave of his chest seemed to send another jolt of pain coursing through him. His breathing was labored now and the pain was growing worse, but both of them knew there was nothing Longarm could possibly do that would ease him.

It was nearly daylight, in that hour shortly before dawn when so many seem to lose their hold on the spark of life, when Lee finally died.

Longarm would have told him that he had done himself proud almost to the end and that he had died well, but that was no longer possible.

When it was over, Longarm swore and began gathering his things together. He was going to have to make a detour to the nearest town, where he could arrange for the burial of Lee and Bobby Trulock and the disposition of their gear.

"Life can be a bitch, horse," he said as he rode west toward where he thought Fountain should be.

# Chapter 7

Ignacio Morales's widow and infant son lived in a sod house
on the nearly flat prairie that had begun the long, gentle
slope down toward the Arkansas flowing out of the mountains toward the distant Mississippi. The land was much
more level here, nearly devoid of the buttes and rocky out-
croppings that were common just a few miles to the north.
Even the grasses here were different, bunch grasses and
soapweed and scatterings of tiny cacti, while to the north
the ground was covered largely with edible forage. It was
somewhere around here—no one but a fool would ever try
to define it precisely—that the Northern Plains ended and
the Great Southwestern Desert began. Longarm idly wondered if he should pick a spot and use it as a definition

between the two great stretches of completely dissimilar grasslands. He was feeling like something of a fool lately anyway, particularly since no one seemed interested in shooting at him in his role as a horse hunter.

Conchita Morales was a plump and not-too-bright young woman with an infant who must have been at least a yearling still nuzzling hungrily at her breast. She welcomed Longarm into the one room of her home, guided him to a seat of honor at the homemade table that dominated the small room, and opened her tattered blouse to let the child nurse.

"Tell me what happened to your husband," Longarm said.

Señora Morales may or may not have understood the question. She began pouring out a rapid flow of Spanish that went far beyond the few words Longarm understood and at three times the rate he might have been able to comprehend even if he had known the words.

"Whoa, ma'am, please!" He held a hand up, and she stopped. "Do you speak English, ma'am?"

*"Sí."*

*Right. You bet,* he thought. *"Si" is the proper answer to that question.* Out of respect for the woman's bereavement, he hid the exasperation he was beginning to feel.

"Let's start over, ma'am," he said slowly. "Could you tell me what happened to your husband?"

She looked blank.

"Señor Morales," he said. *"Qué?"*

He had opened the floodgates again, and for the second time she spouted hard and fast and incomprehensibly.

Again Longarm held up his hand. "Whoa, ma'am. I'm just not following what you're trying to tell me."

This time she seemed to realize the lack of communication. She pulled the drooling child away from her pap, slung him casually onto her hip, and motioned for Longarm to follow.

She led him to a windmill about two hundred yards from the soddy. Even at that short distance the sod house blended so well with the dried grass and sun-baked soil behind it that it was almost camouflaged. Longarm guessed that the windmill and the earthen stock tank served the needs of the house as well as any livestock. He could see the tracks of the woman in the mud at the base of the tank as well as those of cattle and a burro or a small Spanish mule. Activity in the week or more since Morales was killed had obliterated any traces of the buckskin stud that he might have hoped to find there.

"Try again," he invited.

This time the woman mimed the actions that had taken place. First she was her husband carrying a bucket to the water. Then she was a horse, startled at the tank—it must have been night, Longarm decided, although she gave him no gestures that he understood to make that connection— baring its teeth and charging the man on foot. She acted the part of the horse so well, handing the baby to Longarm in order to do so, that Longarm could almost see the horse charging Ignacio, rearing and striking the man with its fore-feet. Then the woman was once again her husband, throwing an arm up but being struck full in the face by a hoof and crumpling to the ground.

"Did you see it, ma'am? Did you see the horse?" Longarm asked.

She shrugged. She could understand him no better than he was able to understand her. She took the baby from him and let it go back to its meal.

They could not talk, but Longarm could understand pride without the need for words. He allowed her to lead him back into the hovel that was her home and to serve him a teaspoonful of refried beans on a scrap of tortilla before he went on his way.

He felt a little better about the woman after that, though, because she seemed a neat enough housekeeper in spite of her other shortcomings, and there were the remains of a number of cornhusk cigarettes, favored by Mexican va-queros, in a dish beside the bed. The widow Morales would not remain alone for long, he suspected.

Longarm tipped his Stetson to her, drew a smile when

he chucked the little one under the chin, and got the hell out of there. He felt as if he had a long way to go before he would be earning his pay, at this rate.

"That's about all I can tell you about Morales, Marshal. I know it ain't much, but none of us was around at the time."

"There wasn't any official investigation, then?"

"Naw. Accidental death is the way we heard it." The man grinned. "Just as well, too. I ain't real sure if the Morales place is in El Paso or Pueblo County. Wouldn't have known who should investigate it."

Longarm nodded. The fellow was town constable for Fountain and worked part time as an El Paso deputy. He had been of no help at all as far as Longarm's investigation was concerned.

"Well, thank you anyhow."

"Any time."

Longarm left the constable's office and found his way to the better of the two saloons one could choose from in the town.

"Maryland rye," he ordered.

The bartender shook his head. "No such thing here."

"Bourbon?"

"How about corn squeezings?"

"How about a beer, then."

The barkeep delivered a brew without enough life in it to raise a good head and accepted Longarm's money wordlessly. The beer was no better than Longarm had expected, but at least it was wet and reasonably cool. He leaned against the bar and resigned himself to the deprivation of being away from the pleasures of Denver.

"Say, are you the fella that's down here chasing that rogue buckskin?" The question came from a table of drinkers nearby.

"I'm afraid so."

"I hope you get that bastard then."

"Have you lost stock to him too?" Longarm's interest perked up a bit.

64

"You bet I have." The man pulled a chair out at their table. "Come and join us."

Longarm did, and of the four men at the table all but one had lost at least a few head to the raiding stallion.

"I'll tell you the truth, Marshal, if it wasn't for the fact that the damn horse killed Morales I'd kinda admire the ol' son of a bitch. I've seen him work, and he's pretty with his nose down t' the ground and a cow in front of him."

"Have you seen him lately?" Longarm asked.

All of them shook their heads.

"I heard there was somebody, a woman maybe, who was supposed to have seen him."

"I remember something about that too."

"Hell, John, you remember. It was that Crowder woman. What's her name again?"

"I disremember too, but she's still living out east of town the last I heard. See her every once in a while at the general store."

"Could you tell me how to get there?" Longarm asked.

The cowboy shrugged. "Sure. She's a little strange, though, so don't expect nothing from her."

"Strange? How so?"

"Damned Easterner is what she is. Has herself those fancy Eastern ideas like the swells up at Colorado Springs. You'd think none of 'em stink when they shit, they're so fine."

"They don't even allow no saloons in their town," another hand said indignantly. "Fella can't get a drink there no matter how dry he is."

"We show 'em though," the third said. "Make 'em ship all their damn beef in by rail. Vegetables, hay—nobody around here wants anything to do with them. Bunch of damned boiled-shirt dandies up there. We ignore 'em."

"About the Crowder place?" Longarm reminded them.

"It's easy to find. You just..."

Ten minutes later Longarm was on his way.

# Chapter 8

"Deputy marshal? I understand that translates as manhunter in plain language. Still, I shall do my duty and treat you as I would any guest. Come in, by all means."

Longarm was glad enough that she quit talking when she did. The chill in the air was damn near enough to give a man pneumonia. He took his snuff-brown Stetson off and stomped his boots more or less free of ranchyard dirt before he entered the small house. "Thank you, ma'am."

"You may hang your hat there, Marshal, and the gunbelt also, if you please. I do not approve of firearms."

"Somehow, ma'am, that doesn't surprise me."

"You needn't become snippy with me, Marshal."

"No, ma'am." He did as he was asked.

The inside of Catherine Crowder's home was about what one would expect of a homestead cabin. But Catherine Crowder was not exactly what one would expect of a homesteader's wife. Or widow. Longarm understood that her husband had died some months earlier.

Longarm sat where she directed and took a moment to give this odd woman a second glance. She was taller than average and looked painfully thin, although it was hard to tell for sure under the layers of cloth that draped her from throat to floor. Longarm was no judge of ladies' fashions, but he thought her dress looked once fashionable but now out-of-date. It hardly mattered, because as far as he could determine she had no figure to worry about either revealing or concealing.

The woman herself was another matter entirely. In her fine, patrician features he could see a quality that not even a veil could have concealed.

She had delicately molded cheekbones and nose over a primly held but nicely rounded mouth. Her hair, tidily rolled and pinned into a bun, was a shade of deep auburn that showed traces of gray that on this woman was quite attractive. There were no wrinkles on her satin-textured flesh to go with the streaks in her hair, and Longarm would have been hard pressed to come within five years of her age if asked to guess. She was actually more interesting in appearance than beautiful, but it was undeniable that there was an aura of quality about her that made her seem out of place in this crude home.

Her unbending carriage, though, and the open hostility in her eyes whenever she looked his way, did nothing to make Longarm feel like a welcome guest.

"I'm sorry for the intrusion, ma'am, and I will be gone just as quickly as possible," he said.

"Nonsense. I am capable of viewing a sunset, Marshal. I would not turn a stray hound away from my door unfed with nightfall coming on."

"Yes, ma'am." Longarm thought he just might have heard a more graciously extended invitation once or twice in his lifetime. On the other hand, it was a fair distance back to town, and her cooking was undoubtedly better than his own would be. "Thank you," he added lamely.

Mrs. Crowder began fussing with something at her stove. Over her shoulder she said, "You may tend your horse now, Marshal. Put him in the shed, but leave some room for yourself. That is where you will sleep tonight."

"Yes, ma'am," he said again. He got his hat, debated for a split second about the Colt, and decided he should leave it where it was for the sake of peace and harmony. Besides, his Winchester was still in its boot on his saddle. In the unlikely event that he needed a weapon he could use that.

The spread here was really more of a farmstead than a ranch. There was an extensive garden behind the house, fenced off from intruding livestock and with a row of light wire mesh along the bottom to discourage visits from rabbits or other small creatures. The garden was much larger than a single family would have required, so Longarm guessed that the lady was raising vegetables as a cash crop.

There was no sign of beef cattle or even a milk cow on the premises, but there were three large hogs in a pen near the shed. They were well past butchering size and Longarm assumed they must be sows, but a closer look showed them to be barrows. Probably, he thought, her husband had planned to slaughter them before now and she might not know how to do the job herself. It was odd, though, that her neighbors would not have lent a hand. Unless they were not on good terms with her.

He did not know how that might be so. After all, she had such a winning manner about her. He made a face.

In addition to the hogs there was a chicken house built low to the ground. A great many hens and a few roosters wandered underfoot through the yard, making the job of keeping his boot soles clean enough for polite company a rather serious business.

There was a light driving rig parked beside the shed where Longarm bedded his horse, and one of the three stalls was

68

occupied by a short coupled bay horse with very clean lines and a small head. A Morgan, Longarm thought. The breed was a rarity but supposed to be strong and versatile enough for both saddle and plow. Longarm put his borrowed mount in the stall next to the bay and gave himself the enclosure farthest from the pigsty. That would not be nearly far enough away, but there seemed to be no choice about it. It was hell what a man had to go through in the line of duty. He wrinkled his nose. A shift of wind direction would definitely be welcome before he bedded down.

"Nice place you have here," he said politely when he rejoined Mrs. Crowder. He sniffed again, and this time the smell was much more interesting than what he had found outside. Whatever she was fixing for supper, he had an idea he was going to like it.

"Thank you, Marshal."

"I'm only a deputy marshal, ma'am, and you can call me Custis if you like. Or Longarm. Most folks do."

"Thank you, Marshal."

He sighed. "Yes, ma'am." He wondered if this woman was deliberately trying to treat him like a schoolboy caught with a pigtail in his inkwell.

"It will be a few minutes before everything is ready," she said, taking a seat across the table from him. "I assume there is something you want to ask me."

"As a matter of fact, ma'am, there is. It's about a horse that's been running wild around here and carrying people's stock off."

She nodded firmly. "I am aware that you have been sent to assassinate Bucky, Marshal. You should know at the outset that I strongly protest such a barbaric attitude, with or without the dubious value of a badge to justify your cruelty."

Longarm exhaled slowly. "It isn't all that vile, ma'am, I assure you. The horse has killed at least two men and seems to have run off an awful lot of stock. We only want him to quit killing people. And ... you called that rogue *Bucky?*"

69

"I did. That poor animal is as gentle as a kitten. I refuse to believe that he has harmed anyone. With the possible exception of Lewis Chance, who was a drunkard and a cowardly horse-beater."

She did not have to bother adding that in her opinion a man who would beat a horse had no right to live. Her tone of voice made that plain enough.

"The thing is, ma'am, I understand you may have actually seen Buck. After he went wild, that is. Plenty of people know him from before, but I haven't found a soul who's seen him since."

"You were not misinformed, Marshal. I saw Bucky several times after he fled from the abuse he had been subjected to. Right out beside that shed, as a matter of fact."

"When was that, ma'am? If you can remember."

"I remember it quite well. Bucky came here three times, the last being the day before my husband was killed. Henry died on June the fourth; therefore, I last saw Bucky on June third."

That was several months ago, but still it was the latest and the only sighting Longarm had yet been able to confirm. "Would you tell me about the horse, ma'am?"

"I shall tell you nothing that I believe might lead you to find the creature, Marshal, but I shall be glad to tell you what a noble animal he really is."

Longarm managed to keep himself from groaning aloud. *Noble?* Now he understood what those boys back in Fountain had been talking about. Back-east views, for damn sure. He sometimes wondered if all the mush those eastern folks ate for breakfast went to their heads instead of their bellies. Still, it was his job to keep his mouth shut and listen, not to judge. Other people were paid to handle that chore.

"I first saw Bucky standing at my garden fence, Marshal. He appeared to be hungry. I had already heard of his alleged misdeeds, although frankly I must say that I did not believe them then any more than I do now. I maintain that his actions were justifiable self-defense and nothing more."

"Yes, ma'am."

70

"I was on my way out to the shed to feed Satin at the time and had a pail of grain."

*Satin?* Longarm had a few private opinions about the kind of person who tried to make a pet out of a perfectly honest, hard-working animal like a horse. In cow country most hands would comfortably live a lifetime without giving a horse a pet name. If a horse was called anything at all, it was more of an identifying feature than an actual name. Like Buck for any buckskin, not just the particular rogue in question. Or Scarface or One-Ear. Or, most often, a selection of cusswords variable enough to meet any mood or circumstance. But Satin? The woman was obviously the kind who would take a perfectly honorable dog and try to turn it into a lap-warmer.

"Naturally," she went on, "I could not allow an animal to remain hungry."

*Naturally,* Longarm thought. The fact that the horse was standing on a sea of perfectly good forage would not come into it.

"I called to him," Mrs. Crowder said. "When I held the pail out to him he was cautious, but he came to me. I scratched the poor animal's nose while he ate the grain from my pail. I can assure you that he made no threatening gestures. He did not so much as lay his ears back or snort much less try to strike at me.

"Bucky came back twice more, and each time the results were precisely the same. He came whenever I called him and he was better company than most human beings I have seen in this benighted part of the country. Much more friendly.

"The last time he came, my husband returned home while Bucky was still here. The poor horse became agitated at my husband's shout of warning, and he fled. I have not seen Bucky since. Frankly, I suspect that the poor animal is terrified of all men, since it was a man who abused him. I doubt that any woman would have trouble with him. Certainly I had none. And when surprised and driven away, Bucky made no effort to attack my husband. He only ran

71

away to defend himself. And I think it is hideous of you to even consider harming him. He is a *nice* horse, Marshal."

"Yes, ma'am." Longarm wondered if Catherine Crowder might be right about one thing, though. Assuming she was not lying to him—and he would not put it past her if she thought it might discourage him from shooting the horse—the animal just might be unafraid around a woman.

Longarm wondered briefly if Mrs. Crowder would help him. He put that thought aside. It seemed obvious that she would have no part of anything like what he had so tentatively in mind. There would have to be another way.

Moreover, there would have to be a lot more to his job than that. Finding and shooting a damned rogue horse was nothing more than an excuse. His job—and he was accomplishing nothing toward it, as far as he could tell, to date—was to find the person who had gone into the business of murdering Federal employees. So far Billy Vail's idea of using Custis Long as a piece of bait on a hook looked like a complete bust.

But that was the way it went sometimes.

"Something seems to be boilin' over on your stove, ma'am," Longarm said.

Mrs. Crowder gave out a short yelp of surprise—it made her seem just a little bit more human to him—and darted off to take the offending pot away from the heat and move it to a cooler section of stovetop, at the back of the surface.

She served the meal a minute or two later, and Longarm found that it tasted as good as it had smelled. It was a stew of sorts, served in bowls, with plates of vegetables on the side and a loaf of really excellent bread to sop up the juices.

It actually took Longarm a minute to realize what was missing, because the stew tasted so good.

"If you're out of meat, ma'am, I'd be glad to help out. Find you an antelope maybe, or draw one of those hogs out there. I know it can't be easy for a woman alone."

*"Marshal!* Please!" She made a face of great distaste. "I do *not* eat the flesh of innocent animals."

"But . . . ?" He pointed vaguely toward the hog pen and the chicken shed outdoors.

"Those pigs were my husband's doing, not mine. The chickens supply eggs, which I sell in addition to my garden produce. I have no use for the pigs, of course, but if I sold them it would only be for someone else to slaughter. I cannot have that on my conscience."

"Yes, ma'am." He should have known that. He swirled his spoon through the thick broth of the stew and found only an assortment of corn and tomatoes and okra and other garden truck. Funny, he thought, the stuff did not taste nearly so good now as it had a few minutes earlier.

He finished it, though, and sat back at least partially satisfied. He did not really want to get back onto the subject of the buckskin rogue nor any other innocent animal, so to make conversation he asked about the lady's now deceased husband. After all, he reasoned, it was almost impossible to find a woman who did not want to talk about her troubles.

"My husband was shot to death in a barroom brawl, Marshal," she said, without a trace of self-pity or of compassion, in her firm, thin-lipped way. "Actually, that implies false conclusions about Mr. Crowder. He was a good enough man. It had been an arranged marriage, and he did his best to make a good husband, as I did mine to perform as a dutiful wife. Now he is gone and I am perfectly content to remain alone."

"You said he was killed in June?"

"Yes. The day after I last saw Bucky." From her tone Longarm could not decide which loss had been the greater, Mr. Crowder or Bucky.

"I am told he was in a place of refreshment in Monument, if you know where that is."

Longarm nodded. He had the acquaintance of a young waitress there, even if she had never told him her name.

"According to the accounts I received, Mr. Crowder was speaking with some friends when for no reason a ruffian began to strike him and to accuse him of cowardice. Mr.

73

Crowder had a shotgun with him, which he commonly carried in the hope of finding a prairie fowl for the dinner table. He lifted the weapon, and witnesses said they believed he intended not to shoot but merely to leave before a fight developed. The other man took that opportunity to shoot him down."

"That sounds awfully strange, ma'am," Longarm observed. Barroom fights were common enough, and Longarm had seen enough strange things happen between men that he was willing to believe almost anything. But still, shootings were not nearly as common as Ned Buntline would like the gullible to believe. Especially shootings for no apparent reason. Longarm was bright enough to realize that there was always *some* reason for murder, whether that reason was known or not.

It seemed most unlikely that there could be any connection between Crowder's death and this case, but a man never knew. And Longarm's interest had been piqued.

"If you like, ma'am, I'll look into it if I get up that way again."

"That would serve no useful purpose at this point, Marshal. The local law officers have already ruled that the shooting was self-defense, because Mr. Crowder did take up his shotgun."

"Yes, ma'am." Longarm had his own opinions about local law enforcement, too. There were good and bright men among them, but not always. He still thought he might take a look into it. And he would not really mind an excuse to look up that pretty little waitress again. It was beginning to bother him that he did not know the girl's name.

"If you will excuse me, ma'am, I reckon I will turn in now. It's been a long day."

"As you wish, Marshal."

Sure was a cold woman, he thought as he retrieved his hat and gunbelt. He would be glad enough to find warmer company.

# Chapter 9

She smiled prettily. "Birgita Hansen," she answered his question.

"Funny," he said, "you don't talk like a Norska."

Again that pretty smile. "Second generation. You should hear my folks." She rolled her eyes. "I have trouble understanding them myself when they try to speak English. Back home our farm was way out of town, though, and I had to board to go to school. That's probably what made the difference in my accent."

"Probably." He looked her over and very much liked what he saw, as he had the first time. "If you'd like someone to walk you home tonight..."

"I think I would like that, even though Randy hasn't

bothered me since the last time you were here. A girl just never knows, and it does pay to be safe."

"I agree completely," Longarm said. "Randy, I take it, is our mutual acquaintance?"

"Uh-huh. Randolph Walters, he calls himself."

"Why'd you put it that way?" he asked.

The girl shrugged. "Just an impression. Sometimes he doesn't answer when someone calls him Randy. I guess that's it. Anyway, a lot of men change their names around here. Not too long ago I saw a boy I used to know back home in Minnesota, but he's carrying a different name now. I don't know why."

Longarm nodded. The habit was as common as Birgita thought, and it did nothing to make the task of law enforcement easier. Oddly enough, though, once a man was caught he usually wanted to be buried under his true name. Quite a few came clean about their pasts when they knew they were on their way to the gallows.

He paid for his lunch and looked around the room. There were too many paople at the tables for any open display of affection for the girl, so he gave her a wink and left. He was looking forward to the chore of walking her home again.

The town was too small to have many drinking places. The lone saloon was attached to the side of the general store and was apparently run by the same family. It was not the sort of place one would normally associate with violent men. It was also not very busy. Longarm introduced himself to the bartender, who gave his name as Norm, and ordered a beer. He had scant hope of finding any Maryland rye here.

"Have you been here long?" Longarm asked the barkeep.

"A while now."

"Would you happen to have been here a few months back when a man named Crowder was shot?"

"Henry? Sure was. I was right here behind this counter, and Henry and a few of the boys were at that table over there having a beer and a talk." He shook his head. "Never could figure out what got that business started, and a man don't hardly ask questions like that of the survivor."

76

"Tell me about it," Longarm prompted.

Norm picked up a towel and mug and began polishing the glass with a distant look of memory on his broad face.

"It ain't all that hard to remember," he said. "We don't get much of that kind of thing around here. Good folks in these parts mostly, and not the troublesome kind. As I remember it, Henry had come in with a load of something to deliver—my wife would remember if it's important, because she does that kind of buying while I tend to this side of the place—and stopped in for his usual beer.

"He got to talking with—let's see, I think it was Bert Taylor and Russ Johnston and someone else, I'm not sure who. Anyhow, I remember they'd got to talking about that buckskin killer horse that was playing hell with the stock growers in the area. He hadn't been at it too awful long then, and Bert had lost some cows to him and was complaining that somebody oughta shoot the son of a bitch.

"Henry was saying he wasn't so sure about that because his own missus had been hand-feeding the damn horse. Said he'd seen it himself just the other day and seen it eat out of her hand, practically."

That sure seemed to prove at least that Mrs. Crowder had not been lying for the sake of saving the horse. She might have reason to lie to a deputy marshal about it, but her husband obviously had not shared her tenderhearted Eastern view about livestock and he would have had no reason to lie to his cronies about the horse. Longarm filed the information away in his memory for future reference.

"Henry started to say something about the horse running away from something, but he never said what it was the killer had run from because before he got any further old Randy begun cussing him and moving in on him. Loud, he was, and damned mean about it. Nasty mean. He was saying things that there wouldn't hardly be no man could walk away from without a fight. Then Henry picked his shotgun up by the barrel, and Randy drew on him."

"Randy? That would be . . . ?"

"Randy Walters. But I ain't telling anything on him,

77

Marshal. It's all public record. Least I figure it must be. It never come to trial or anything like that, but the local deputy looked into it and talked to all of us that'd been in the place and he said it was self-defense and there wouldn't be any charges. The way I understand it now there can't be any charges filed because he's once cleared. Double something or other?"

"Double jeopardy," Longarm said automatically. As a matter of fact, that law applied only when a person was acquitted of a formal charge. Since no charge had ever been filed for the man to be absolved of, a legal charge could still be properly filed. There was no Federal law involved, so actually it was none of Longarm's business. Still, he did not see any reason to mention that Walters could still be brought to trial for the shooting of Henry Crowder.

Of more interest to Longarm at the moment was the fact that the man who had done the shooting was Randolph Walters. The man was a bully at the least and probably a murderer as well.

Longarm thanked the bartender, finished his beer, and wandered out to see the sights of Monument. There were few enough of those that interested him, although the Denver and Rio Grande ran excursion train specials down to the area so the city folks from Denver could hire rigs and drive out to a nearby lake for picnics and lawn parties. Much of the town's business came from catering to the needs of those day visitors.

Several others in town confirmed the bartender's version of the Crowder shooting, although none in as much detail. Longarm doubted there would be enough error in what he had already been told to justify the trouble of looking up the deputy who had investigated the shooting. His judgment on that, he realized, was influenced to some extent by the fact that he had already decided he would not like the son of a bitch if he did get around to meeting him. Longarm had the feeling that Randolph Walters had gotten away with murder.

Longarm frittered the afternoon away with some desultory conversations and a stop at the general store to replenish his supply of cheroots, matches, and other things. He had no luck finding any Maryland rye in the town.

Supper—he made it a point to arrive earlier this time—was fried steak and fried potatoes and half a gallon of brown gravy rich with meat drippings. After the previous night's vegetable stew, the meal was good. But it was his dessert, after leaving the restaurant, that he expected would be the real treat.

He walked home with Birgita, knowing the way this time and comfortable with the girl.

"No unpleasant intrusions this time," he said as he opened the door for her.

"Apparently there won't be any more either," she said.

"What do you mean?"

She trailed a fingernail across his belly as she moved past him to enter the dark hallway. "I overheard some of my customers talking this evening. I'm a terrible eavesdropper, you know. Anyway, they were saying they had seen Randy in a lather this afternoon. Said he got his horse out of the livery without even asking for any money back on the board bill he'd paid ahead of time and went to the boarding house and cleaned out all his things. Never stopped for a refund there either, they were saying. Then he jumped on his horse and headed out of town at a gallop." She grinned. "Maybe he heard my protector was back in town."

Longarm could make no sense out of that. He had made no secret about the fact that he was asking questions about the Crowder shooting, but Walters had already been cleared of that. And surely the man would know that a penny-ante shootout in a small town was not a Federal offense. He shook his head. There probably was no connection there at all, so there was no point worrying about it. A man could paint himself into any number of corners by making assumptions. And at the moment he had other things to think about. Like a very pretty girl with long, golden hair.

He followed Birgita down the hallway and felt more than saw her stop at her own door. She opened it—no one was much given to the use of locks when you got outside the big-city influence of Denver—and struck a match. A moment later she had the lamp lighted, and Longarm closed and locked the door behind him.

She came into his arms willingly and raised her face for his kiss.

Her breathing changed and became more rapid, and he could feel her fingers busy at his buttons. She sank to the floor so she could work at his fly buttons at a more comfortable level. Or perhaps she had a better reason than that for being down there.

She had a better reason, he discovered quickly.

"My oh my," he observed, "you do seem to have the busiest tongue in town."

"Is that a complaint?"

"Not hardly. I'm in no hurry."

"Good." She went back to what she had been doing.

After a time—he really was in no hurry for her to stop—she rose to her feet, and Longarm helped her out of her dress. She was far prettier without her clothes than with them. Her breasts were full and globular above the visible tracery of her ribcage. Her nipples were tiny and of such a light pink that it took close examination to tell where the pale skin of her breast stopped and the aureolae began. Longarm was willing to make that close examination. Her nipples looked virginal, he thought.

If her breasts were virginal, the rest of her was not. She had little pubic hair and what there was of it was a scanty nest of soft, golden curls. Droplets of moisture clung to the curls. He examined that too.

She was already prepared for him and after only a moment she pulled him on top of her and opened herself to him. He entered her slowly, and a sweet smile tugged at her lips. She closed her eyes.

Longarm stroked gently until he felt her hips begin to writhe and to move with him. Her breath was coming in short, quick gasps, and she began to knead the slabs of firm muscle on his back with work-hardened hands. He was glad she did not have long fingernails, or he would have been sliced raw.

Birgita's neck arched and her body stiffened beneath his slow thrusts. She bit her lip and quivered as she stifled a cry of pleasure.

She relaxed and lay limp with her arms still circling him. "No wonder I was hoping you'd come back," she whispered.

"Which is exactly why I came back," he said into her ear. It was not really a lie. Or not much of one.

"But you haven't..."

Longarm smiled. "I told you already, I'm in no hurry."

Birgita sighed. She nuzzled into his neck and began to kiss his jaw. Longarm began to stroke into her again, slowly at first and then with more insistence, feeling her move beneath him and gauging his own actions to meet her rising responses.

Later, hours later, they lay together in a comfortable, somnolent silence. Distantly he heard the girl sigh and felt her press the flat of her palm against his chest.

It was so pleasant...

Longarm sat bolt upright in the rumpled bed, startling the girl and bringing them both wide awake.

"Son of a bitch!" he hissed. *"Randolph!"*

"Randy? What about him?"

"No, damn it, not Randy. And not Walters either. I *knew* there was something familiar there, but it took me a while to get it. There isn't any picture, just a description. I'm sure of it, though."

"You aren't making any sense, Custis."

"Oh, yes, I am. Your friend Randy is wanted in New Mexico Territory for suspicion of murder for hire. State of Texas, too, if I remember correctly. But the name on the papers isn't Randy Walters, it's Walter Randolph. *Damn,* I feel like an idiot. I had him right in my hands. Had my gun on him, even. And I let him walk away. He must be laughing up his sleeve tonight."

Longarm shook his head. If only it had come to him before.

81

He forced himself to forget about it and lay back beside the girl. There would be time enough to think about Walter Randolph in the morning. At the moment he was exhausted.

# Chapter 10

Longarm sent his wire before breakfast, ate well, and collected his horse from the shed behind the rooming house where Birgita lived. By the time he was done he had his answer. Walter Randolph was a hired gun, a specialist with the rifle and shotgun instead of short arms. Among a number of local wants, Randolph was accused of shooting a Cherokee policeman in the Indian Nation. Deputy Marshal Long should apprehend the fugitive if Randolph was encountered.

Longarm gave a thin-lipped smile of self-deprecation. It was a bit late for that now. He thought about lighting a cheroot, but rejected the idea. He had been trying to cut down anyway. He sighed and mounted the waiting horse.

"Marshal?"

"Yeah?" He remembered seeing the man in the saloon the afternoon before, but he did not know his name.

"Thought you might wanna know. I heard last night that the buckskin horse you're looking for carried some cows off from the Lazy P the day before yesterday. One of their hands was bitching about it."

Longarm nodded. "Thanks."

Two days after the fact was the closest he had yet come to the horse. He turned his mount toward the Lazy P.

The foreman Brent was there when Longarm arrived. "Step down, Marshal. You missed dinner, but we can find something for you if we look hard enough."

"No thanks, I ate already." It had been only a strip of hard jerky eaten from the saddle, but it was enough. "I understand you had a loss to the buckskin."

"Maybe old Buck forgot this is where his troubles started, or something. He wasn't all that close to the headquarters anyhow. Was kinda out toward the fringe of the grass we use." Brent squinted toward the sun, which was already dropping toward the rim of mountains to the west. "It's two, three hours out there if you were wanting to look it over."

"I was."

"If I was you, Marshal, I'd wait until morning. It's a long ride. Besides, that way I could send Handy out with you. Don't know as you could find it by yourself, and Handy knows the horse and our range better than just about anybody you could name."

"I appreciate your help," Longarm said.

"Hell, Marshal, you're out here trying to help *us,* aren't you?"

He gave Brent a tight smile. "Not everybody sees it that way, but yes."

The foreman shrugged. "Anything we can do, just name it."

"I'll be glad to accept your offer, then."

"Good enough. You can offsaddle an' turn your horse into that pen over there. There's some empty bunks you can throw your gear on." He grinned. "You'll know when the grub is ready by the sound of the stampede."

They pulled the horses from a road jog down to a walk and let them plod at the easier pace through the soft sand of a dry wash. Just beyond it on a slightly higher bench where the equipment would not be washed out in the spring thaw or by flash floods there was a windmill and galvanized steel water tank. A line of low hills followed the course of the dry streambed for a half mile or so. The shallow well had been drilled close enough to the usually dry bed to capture any underground water following the same unnoticeable downslope of land.

"Right by this tank it was," Handy said.

"Any tracks?"

The old cowhand shrugged. "I wasn't out here to look for myself, but Tom said he didn't see much."

"Tom would be the man who saw where the stock had been run off?" Longarm asked.

"Uh-huh." They reached the tank and pulled to a halt, letting their horses drop their noses to drink if they wished. Handy reached into a pocket for his pipe and began to load it. "You got a picture of Tom in your pocket as I recall. Tom Morris. He's the one found it. Said he could see where Buck picked four head out of a bunch that'd come up to water and drove them off acrost that hill. Said he couldn't find any tracks to follow outside the muddied ground right by the tank here."

Longarm searched the ground around them, but he knew the effort was futile before he began. There was little ground that was softened enough by spilled water to take a decent hoofprint, and what there was was churned up twice daily by the cattle coming in to water. Off to one side he could see the imprint of a shod horse, but there was only the single track. There was no way he could determine if it might have been left by the buckskin, by Tom Morris's horse, or by any other rider's mount. A tracker would have had to arrive within a matter of hours after the loss to make any sense from the much-used patch of ground. And beyond the moist circle around the tank, the ground was baked adobe hard.

"You say Morris already checked over the ridge there?"

"That's what he said."

"I think I'd like to take a look myself, anyway."

Handy nodded and took a draw on his pipe. The burning leaf sputtered and sizzled faintly, and the smoke smelled good in the clean, fresh air.

If a pipe tasted half as good as it smelled, Longarm thought, he might switch from his cheroots.

"I expect I'd do that too in your shoes, Marshal. If you don't mind, though, I'll wait here." He made a sour face. "Brent asked me to check the grease on the mill gears, so I expect I gotta climb up there soon or late. It's a bitch what a man has to do these days so's he can go on pretending that he works horseback."

Longarm smiled. He understood Handy's problem. When Handy had been young there was only open range and whatever water and forage nature provided. Now the cattle business was changing, becoming a real business, complete with stock issues and dividends. The advent of the windmill, providing water where the grass had been useless for a thousand years, was only the start of it. Some cowmen were already beginning to cut hay for winter feed, hoping to reduce winter losses for their stockholder owners. A few had begun to use fences to block off water access or create holding pastures for calves or market steers. The business was in a state of change, and few of the new methods involved work that could be done from horseback. Men like Handy could expect to find themselves on their feet more and more as the years went on, Longarm suspected. And, apparently, the old man did not like it, but at least he seemed willing to accept it.

"You do what you need. I'll poke around over there and be back in an hour or so."

"Take your time, Marshal. We won't get back in time to accomplish any useful work today anyhow, and I'd as

86

soon be out here as smelling the blankets in the bunkhouse."

Longarm nodded and bumped his horse into a lope.

The ridge Longarm mentioned was scarcely more than a rise. From a distance it would hardly be noticeable, but the land here rolled and swelled deceptively. Back in the used-to-be times, a traveler, even an Army officer, new to the country might think he could see anything that was moving for miles around because of the apparent openness of the ground. Yet a wagon train, a troop of cavalry, or half the Southern Cheyenne nation might be a quarter of a mile away. That had led to difficulties more than once.

Longarm topped the low swell and stopped to survey the grass. There was a faint tracery of bunchgrasses that might, or as easily might not, have been disturbed by the passage of an animal. A cow more than likely would have followed a lower and easier route to the water, so there was at least the possibility that a horse had passed this way. Or an antelope or a wandering mule deer. Longarm sighed and set out with faint hope that he would find any tracks but unwilling to miss a clue through the laziness of negative assumptions. Most law work, he had long since found, was plain and simple boring.

He rode forward slowly for twenty minutes or more and startled a small band of pronghorn antelope into sudden motion as he topped another hill above where they were browsing. His line of travel took him to the spot where a doe had been lying with a nursing youngster at her side. Longarm was neither pleased nor surprised to see that she had left no trace of her passage on the hard ground she had vacated not two minutes before.

He shook his head and pulled a cheroot from his vest pocket. If he could not find any trace of a pronghorn he had *seen* leave the spot, he damn sure was not going to find any decent trace of a horse that might or might not have come this way days before. It was time to go back.

There was one good thing about this part of the country, he mused as he rode back the way he had come. It would be difficult for even a New York city boy to get lost here.

The mountains were always south to north, and the harsh, rocky jut of Pike's Peak dominant in the center of the range.

He removed his Stetson to wipe a sheen of sweat from his forehead. Hot as it was down here, on top of that peak the wind would be cold and invigorating. From this distance he could see no snow on its bare, rocky cap, but there would still be ice and perhaps a bit of crusted snow to be found in the shadowed cracks and crevices up there. A snowfield would be damned welcome now, or a drink of the icy-cold running snowmelt that flowed down from the mountains. Down here there was only sun-heated tepid water in the stock tanks. The thought made him thirsty, and he took a lukewarm swallow from his canteen.

Longarm topped the last rise and stopped above the windmill and tank. A few cattle had drifted in and were grouped around the tank, and Handy's horse was cropping grass, ground-reined, a few yards away.

He had to look for a moment before he saw the old man himself, and he was surprised. Handy seemed to be a hard-working type, not much given to loafing on the job, yet the old fossil was stretched out in the scant shade offered by the windmill tower.

*Probably finished his job and is just waiting,* Longarm thought.

He rode closer and thought about sneaking up on the old boy and giving him a scare. It would pay him back for that heated-plate business. And there was no man who could admit to any resentment of horseplay or practical jokes and still stay in the same bunkhouse with a bunch of rowdy hands. The poor fellow might *feel* resentment, but he sure wouldn't dare show it.

On the other hand that might be a bit beneath the supposed dignity of a deputy United States marshal. Longarm rode on in and felt a twinge of disappointment, because he could so easily have gotten away with a joke. Handy must be sleeping soundly; he never stirred when Longarm rode up to him.

88

There would be no jokes. And Handy was not going to stir. Not now. Not ever.

The iron-gray hair on Handy's head was matted with dark blood, and the old man's skull was badly indented. There was no question that the old cowhand was dead.

Longarm felt a sense of deep loss and anger. He dismounted and knelt to begin reading sign before he approached the body.

# Chapter 11

"Oh, that miserable son of a bitch of a killer horse," Brent moaned. The foreman clenched his fists in his rage, and the muscles of his neck and jaw stood out like whipcord as he clenched his teeth, but there was no way he could vent his frustration and anger. "I wish..." He shook his head violently. "I don't know what I wish. *Damn it!*"

"He was a damned good man," Longarm agreed.

The Lazy P hands had gathered around and were gawking at the body Longarm had brought in, some with sympathy and some with only the morbid curiosity that will draw a crowd to a train wreck.

Handy's skull had been crushed, although most of the blood had come from his mouth and nose and eye sockets.

He would have to be washed thoroughly before he could be laid out for viewing and burial.

Longarm had already checked, though, distasteful as the task was, and there was a curving ridge within the indentation of the massive wound that could only have come from an iron horseshoe. Longarm had even found the puncture that would have resulted from the toe caulk on the shoe.

"It was most likely an accident, the way I read it," Longarm said. "The ground had been marked up some by the cattle that were milling around there, but the way I see it Handy was on his horse at the time. He was riding a mare, for some reason."

Brent nodded. "Damned ol' bitch never has took. Exposed her I don't know how many times, but she's just no good for breeding. We couldn't sell her as a regular mare, of course, because nobody could use her for a brood mare, but Handy was kinda partial to her, liked the way she moved. He broke her out and used her now and then for a saddle horse when there was ground to cover. She isn't smart enough to work off of."

Longarm had wondered about that. Few cowhands were willing to be seen riding a mare. Few, for that matter, wanted anything to do with a stallion. A gelding was day-in-and-day-out dependable, without the breeding urges that can turn a windborne scent into a total loss of interest in the work at hand. Apparently Handy was an exception. Certainly he had proven himself far beyond the point of caring what other people thought when he put a saddle onto an animal.

"Anyway," Longarm continued, "there were some marks that might have been where a horse reared up. The way I see it, one possibility is that the buckskin stud came up behind the mare and tried to mount her. She isn't in season—I checked. So she'd resent the stud and want to fight him. If Handy was on her when the stud tried to get up onto her, well..."

"That don't sound like Handy," Brent said. "That old boy knew the mare, and he knew the stud. He damn sure

91

knew enough to leave the saddle, even if he was stupid enough to let a wild stud get that close behind him. And I doubt that, too."

"It could be," Longarm said, "that he thought he knew the buckskin well enough not to have to be cautious around him. Hell, there's more farmers killed each year by their pet milk-bred bulls than there are cowhands killed by wild stock."

"Handy wasn't no damned farmer, and he knew as much as any man how to handle stock, cows or horses, either one. That old boy was canny," Brent said.

Longarm sighed. "I know. But I sure don't have any other explanation. If you come up with one, I'd sure like to know about it."

Brent started to say something, then snapped his mouth closed. "Reckon I don't, at that, Marshal. It sure don't sound like Handy, but I don't see any other way to figure it, any more than you do. It's for damn sure it was a horseshoe that caved his head in like that. I just don't know what else to say."

Longarm nodded. He did not mention it, but he had had the same doubts, and had gone over every square inch of Handy's body before he brought the old man home. Longarm had been convinced there must be a bullet or knife wound, some marks of strangling, *some* damn thing. But there was not. There was only that massive, ugly wound caused by a striking hoof. The evidence was plain, and there was no point in arguing with the facts even, or especially, when they do not coincide with the investigator's preconceived notions.

"Boys," Brent said, standing and turning to his crew, "from now on there isn't to be a man riding out of this place without a rifle slung to his saddle. Anybody see that damn Buck, he's to shoot the son of a bitch and bring me his ears. I mean it, now. Anybody sees that horse and doesn't shoot, well, he doesn't have a place at the Lazy P for five minutes more. You understand that?"

The men nodded. Most of them looked as angry and

upset as their foreman. Brent was literally shaking, but there was nothing more he could do about it.

"If you don't mind," Longarm said, "I'll stay the night here and then head for the nearest telegraph. I expect I'd better report this."

The foreman seemed only marginally aware. "You do that, Marshal. Nearest wire would be over to Colorado Springs, I reckon."

One of the cowhands spat. It was Tom Morris, the cowboy who had been in the picture with Lew Chance and the buckskin horse. "Bunch of damned swells over there, Marshal. You'd be better off going up to Monument. Better folks. Nobody around here has any truck with them dandies at the Springs."

Personal preference, spelled Birgita, would have sent Longarm to Monument too, but a sense of duty said he should go to the closest telegraph office, not the one where he had a warm and pretty companion close to hand.

The town, more of a city in miniature really, was an exception for this part of the country. The streets were wide and carefully laid out, the houses Eastern mansions on an only slightly smaller scale, trees and ornamental plantings well established and carefully tended if still far from old enough to be mature. The place had an air of wealth about it and was extraordinarily clean. There was no refuse in the streets, and even the rubbish bins were hidden in the alleys. Longarm was impressed.

He was also glad he still had part of a bottle of Maryland rye in his saddlebags because, as the boys at the Lazy P had warned him, there were no saloons to be seen anywhere in the city. Liquor was forbidden here, although he understood that the working classes and shopkeepers could tank up a few miles away in Colorado City.

There was no time for side ventures at the moment, though, and Longarm headed for the railroad depot off Pikes Peak Avenue below the ornate Antlers Hotel.

The operator got his wire off, collect to Billy Vail, and

Longarm told him he would stop back in a few hours in case there was an answer. Billy did not particularly like his deputies to be out of touch for too long a time.

With that chore out of the way, there was nothing for Longarm to do but pass the time until any return message should be received. It was not yet noon but close enough that he might expect a hotel restaurant to be serving lunch, so he left his horse at the station and walked up the hill to The Antlers. The sun felt good on his back, and he enjoyed the short walk.

The hotel lobby was dark and heavily furnished, its woodwork carved and the gilt lead ceiling panels ornate. The lights, incredible for such an out-of-the-way area, were electrified instead of the far more common gas. Longarm was impressed.

It was still too early for hunger to send him into the dining room, so he took a seat in one of the plush lobby chairs and lighted a cheroot.

"Custis?" He turned toward the source of the thin, hesitant voice. "I declare, it *is* you."

Longarm stood and swept his hat off. He was able to keep from laughing out loud, but he was unable to suppress the smile that memory brought to his lips. He kept remembering the young lady underneath his bed with her nose pressed into the dustballs and Billy Vail sitting practically on top of her.

"This is a pleasant surprise, Brenda."

The congressman's daughter was dressed quite differently from the last time he had seen her. She looked cool and elegant now, as did the matronly woman Brenda was strolling with.

"Mrs. Spencer," Brenda said, "may I present United States Marshal Custis Long of Denver. Marshal, Mrs. Spencer."

"A pleasure, ma'am, but the lady exaggerates. I'm only a deputy marshal."

Brenda said, "It makes no difference."

"To the Justice Department it does."

94

"Mrs. Spencer, would you mind if I joined you later? I want to ask the marshal about some mutual friends in the Denver political arena." She smiled prettily. "It's all non-sense to me, but Daddy seems to think it's important, for some silly reason."

"Of course, dear." The matron bobbed her head and moved regally away.

"Now, Marshal, if you would be so good as to join me in my suite?"

Longarm followed her. He waited until they were behind the closed door of her sitting room—proper enough since the bedchamber was separate—before he broke into a grin and said, "Dandy little liar, aren't you?"

"Dear Custis, that is the *nicest* thing you have ever told me! I think it's a lovely compliment, and I thank you." With an impish grin she dropped all pretense and moved into his arms, raising her face for his kiss and returning it hungrily.

"Been lonesome down here, has it?" he teased when they came up for air.

Brenda made a pout. "You wouldn't *believe* how stuffy the good ladies can be. Seeing you was like a breath of fresh air. Honestly!" she shuddered.

Longarm did not believe her melodramatics for a moment, but it was nice to see her anyway.

"Are you down here on that business Marshal Vail was telling you about?" She laughed. "I couldn't help over-hearing all of it, you know. Tell me all about it." She paused, but went on before he could answer. "No, not now. We can talk later if there is time. Right now..."

She began undoing the long row of incredibly tiny buttons that began at her throat and extended to waist level on her gown. "This is going to take quite enough time as it is, just getting out of this stupid thing and all that goes with it. I swear, Custis, sometimes I envy the freedom the lower classes exhibit. A shirtwaist and skirt is enough to cover one's limbs. The rest of it is just so much bother."

Complaints or not, Longarm noticed, Brenda had no

trouble ridding herself of the encumbrances, and a moment later she stood naked and eager, ready for another kiss. And more.

As a Federal employee more or less under the young lady's father's command, Deputy Marshal Long could hardly do less than comply with her requests. It was only the dutiful thing to do.

Longarm performed his duty with a will.

The haughty young lady, so proper and reserved in the drawing room, was a delightfully wanton hussy in bed.

Her lips and tongue were a searing flame that burned him from earlobe to toe, lingering often and well at the points between.

She gave and she demanded to be given to, and Longarm joined her in the frenzy of her efforts.

When the first rush of desire had been sated she was unwilling to stop or even to slow her efforts.

"There. Yes. Oh. Again, Custis, there. Yes." She wiped her mouth inelegantly on the corner of a pillowcase, rolled onto her stomach, and tugged him on top of her.

At first Longarm did not understand what she wanted. It was no pretense. He genuinely did not expect such a thing from a high-born young lady, regardless of her previous conduct.

"I might hurt you," he protested.

She giggled. "I'm not *weird*, darling, and you *won't* hurt me. I happen to *like* this."

Longarm was not so sure. But, what the hell, duty is duty. As gently as he could, he did as Brenda asked.

*How about that*, he asked himself shortly. Maybe there were hidden advantages to some of the things a man wouldn't normally think of on his own. The truth was, he had not felt anything that tight—or that eager—in a long, long time.

"That, darling," she said when their breathing had begun to slow and the sweat was drying on his chest, "accounts for two of the three possibilities. Would you care to make it a clean sweep?"

Longarm's answer was a smile.

* * *

Later—it worked out quite nicely, really, because by then the hour was more suitable for luncheon—he escorted her to the dining room, at least as ornate as the lobby and decorated in the dark woods and flocked velvet wallpaper.

Brenda waved or spoke to at least half of the people seated in the large dining room, and Longarm felt uncomfortably aware of the eyes upon them. He helped Brenda to a seat and accepted the waiter's assistance with his own chair.

The menu showed a selection ranging from fresh brook trout to broiled lobster. Brenda ordered oysters on the half shell and pressed duck. Longarm did not think Billy would like seeing that little item on his expense sheet, so it looked like he was going to be stuck with a bill of his own. In the higher social circles, he thought, a willing romp could be a damn sight more expensive than a night in the best cathouse in Denver.

"I don't see it on here," Longarm said when his guest's order had been duly noted, "but do you think the cook could rassle up some fried steak for me, with maybe a big ol' potato and the fixings to wet it all down?"

The waiter gave him a wink along with an assurance that that was indeed possible.

When it came the meat was done precisely the way Longarm liked it and was as good as anything he had put a tooth to in quite some time. The clientele, Longarm decided, might be swells from the East, but the chef here was a good old boy from the interesting side of the Big Muddy.

It was with a sense of contented well-being that Longarm lit his cigar, an excellent leaf furnished by the management, and allowed the young lady to persuade him that her father really did need additional information that they could best discuss in private.

97

# Chapter 12

Longarm thought over the contents of the telegraph message once again as he rode back toward the Lazy P.

Billy Vail was not always the easiest man to work for, but Vail had spent his share of time in the saddle with a gun close to hand and a warrant in his pocket. He knew what it was like in the field, and he was not given to hysterics when some idiot in Washington hollered "jump."

If Billy Vail was beginning to sweat from the pressure that back-East politicians were applying for the solution of this multiple murder—and the tenor of that message damn sure showed that Vail was starting to sweat—then the pressure was hot and heavy indeed.

Billy wanted that murderer found and the case closed right now.

Damn it, Longarm thought, there was just so much a piece of bait could do. From there on it was up to the fish. And so far...

It was almost as if the hidden rifleman had been trailing Longarm's thoughts as well as his horse, as if the man had waited and chosen this precise moment. The bullet did not even come as any great surprise at that instant.

The heavy slug sizzled past Longarm's belly with that peculiar zipping drone of sound that was so quickly present and so quickly gone. It passed between Longarm's belly and the horse's reins, somehow managing to miss his arm and rein hand in the process. The rifleman had led his target just a hair too much as the horse moved at a slow jog, and that slight error saved Longarm's life.

The deputy's response was instantaneous, much quicker than it might have been if he had not been thinking along the lines he was and found himself already prepared for the ambush.

He threw himself out of the saddle and to the left, away from the direction the bullet had come from, as if he had been hit and was downed.

It was an old enough trick, probably as old as men sending projectiles at one another, whether bullets, arrows, or thrown rocks. But playing possum became such an ancient trick because it was effective.

Longarm fell heavily onto his side and willed himself not to roll for cover. He lay very nearly as he fell, craning his neck so he would have a field of vision up the slope from which the shot had come.

His horse, reins still draped over its neck, shied at the sudden activity and broke into a hard run for a hundred yards or more before it slowed and finally stopped. It dropped its head to graze, and the reins fell to the ground. Having ground-reined itself, it would likely go no further—although Longarm knew better than to place implicit trust in any animal's training—but the damn thing was carrying Longarm's Winchester in its boot. Waiting to pull the rifle free would have been an immediate giveaway that Longarm was playing possum, and he had not even considered it. Now, though, he was playing a deadly game of hide and seek with only his belly gun and derringer to defend himself from an expert rifleman.

His best bet for survival, Longarm realized, would be for the rifleman to come near to confirm his kill.

Longarm lay motionless, hoping to draw the son of a bitch in.

While he waited he studied the terrain as well as he was able by moving only his eyes. He did not dare move his head or the ambusher might see, particularly if he had one of those telescopic sights mounted on his rifle. As he very well might have. The shot had come from an incredible distance if it was fired, as Longarm assumed, from the top of the slight rise.

Immediately around the spot where Longarm lay there was only baked earth and short, dry grass. No brush to hide him nor rocks to protect him, not even any soapweed projecting above the level of the bunch grass.

At least he had one thing to be thankful for. The ground here was devoid of the low, prickly cactus that grew so profusely just a few miles to the south. He had enough problems without having to deal with a buttful of stickers.

He had been riding in a grassy area between two low ridges and not a sandy wash, so there was not even an embankment he could crawl under once the rifleman got as close as he was going to.

Twenty yards to the west, though, there was a small outcropping of chalk-white rock, and beyond that—he could not be sure without moving to get a better view—there seemed to be some irregularities in the surface of the slope. Probably faint washes caused by runoff when the winter snows melted year after year.

Longarm lay still and forced himself to relax.

The sun was like a weight on his face and neck, and a line of sweat pooled beside one eye, trickled across his nose, and ran down into the other eye, where the salt stung and made him blink. He wanted to wipe the unpleasant sting away, but he could not.

He could smell the dust-dry earth and the hot, dry stems of cured grass. His right leg began to cramp, and he could do nothing to ease the pain. A few inches of movement would have been enough. He was not willing to take that risk.

It had been long enough now, he thought, for the rifleman to become impatient and begin to move down the slope.

Another thought came to him and chilled him despite the heat of the strong sunshine.

Longarm might have played his trick *too* quickly. The rifleman might be assuming that the deputy was dead. The bastard might already be riding off, secure in the knowledge that his target had been taken down. By now he could be a mile away.

Longarm bit his lip and stared up the slope until his eyes were smarting from the strain, hoping to see some movement up there that would indicate that the ambusher was still in the area. He was so close. He did not want to lose the bastard now. And it would take too long for him to reach his horse and begin a chase. The rifleman had to be there.

He felt a breeze slip between the slopes to cross his sweaty face with a soothing false chill, and a moment later he saw a hint of motion high on the slope that might have been only the passage of the wind through the grasses.

Yet the grass between Longarm and that uncertain motion had not swayed.

*He's there,* Longarm thought with a sense of triumph and satisfaction that was not at all justified under the circumstances. The distance was still much too great for a handgun to be effective.

A manshape came slowly, cautiously into view at the edge of Longarm's straining vision.

*That's it,* Longarm thought. From where the rifleman had first fired, he had had a clear shot at a man on horseback. But Longarm's fall had placed him below the line of sight.

101

Probably some unnoticed rise in the contour of the slope had intervened. The ambusher had had to move down to take another sight.

The figure stopped moving and settled into one spot.

*Taking his time,* Longarm thought. *Watching for movement. Wanting to make sure before he comes down the rest of the way. Sure, that's reasonable. He . . .*

There was a glint of sunlight on polished metal or glass.

*Aw, shit,* Longarm thought. The rifleman knew his business all too well.

Too well to walk up to an armed man, even a presumed dead armed man. He would sit right there at a range still too far for a Winchester saddle gun and pump a few more rounds into the body, just to make sure.

Longarm cursed himself bitterly. He should have remembered that from the body of Charles Wolfe, the government hunter. Wolfe's murderer never approached his body and left no tracks near him. He had simply killed the unsuspecting hunter and ridden quietly away.

Longarm was already rolling when he saw the faint puff of smoke rise from the far-shooting rifle. He rolled aside, and a moment later a bullet struck the hard earth at an angle, digging an ugly furrow into the ground and sending small clods flying before it ricochetted off into the distance with a dull smack and a nasty whine.

"Game time's over," Longarm muttered aloud as he came to his feet and threw himself toward the scant protection of the rocks, too many yards away.

Another bullet passed and struck somewhere behind him. This time he heard the shot seconds afterward. He was not aware of any sounds of the gunfire before that shot, although he must have heard it.

He threw himself forward and bellied down behind the rocks, his double-action Colt in his hand, even though he knew full well that the short gun was useful here only as a prop to his own morale. It damn sure was no threat to a target so far away.

*You're in for it now, old son,* he told himself.

102

A bullet sliced fragments of stone from the top of the rock Longarm was lying behind, and another quickly behind it.

"Whatever you're shooting, you son of a bitch, it's no single-shot buffalo gun," Longarm muttered to the distant rifleman.

Another rapidly thrown pair of shots whanged off the stone to confirm Longarm's judgment. There was no man alive who could reload a single-shot weapon that quickly.

Worse, there were damned few men alive who could so consistently hit such a small rock at that distance. Longarm took a quick look around the side of the outcrop. It had to be four hundred yards. Perhaps more.

Longarm had heard probably all the brags there were about long-range shooting. He knew better. A Creedmore target shooter could hit a man-sized target every time at that range and nearly every time at far greater distances. But it took him half an hour to swab and cool his barrel after each shot and minutes more to get his rest and his breathing and his trigger slack exactly right before he touched off the round.

This guy, whoever he was, was throwing his shots with a rabbit hunter's speed and was *still* hitting at distances that would have been at the thin edge of possibility for a man with a saddle gun in his hands.

The bastard was good, Longarm acknowledged without joy.

Longarm shoved his Colt back into the holster at his hip and gathered himself on his knees. The possum game was over, and if he stayed where he was there were only two things that could happen, neither of them good.

One would be that the rifleman would shift position again and put a bullet where he wanted it. Which was *not* where Longarm would want one.

The other thing would be that the man would withdraw and wait to make another, possibly more successful, try again. The second possibility was no more attractive to Longarm than the first. He *wanted* this man.

He gathered himself and waited.

A bullet struck the base of his protective rocks at the right side, and then a second hit somewhere close to the left side. It was what he had been waiting for.

Longarm came up like a sprinter running the dash. He sprang up and out, already at a full run by the time he was erect, and raced for the slightly broken ground above and to the right of the rocks.

Another shot sounded from up on the hill, but Longarm had no idea where the bullet had gone. Even the best rifleman will have trouble with a rapidly moving target, and at such long range a proper lead is almost impossible to judge.

Almost, but not quite.

Another bullet snatched at Longarm's clothing as he threw himself down into a shallow depression that ran haphazardly up the hillside.

Longarm rolled over and checked. He had felt no direct impact, but the son of a bitch had holed Longarm's calfskin vest.

He pressed himself flat against the soil and wriggled out of the vest. He wadded it into a ball and crept up the line of the depression to a likely-looking place where the side of the wash dipped low.

There, carefully, he shoved the vest up against the abrupt slope to a place where he hoped the rifleman would be able to see it.

The man was welcome to think it was the vest with Longarm still inside it or even Longarm's head. The brown of the leather was close enough to the shiny brown of Longarm's hair that a mistake could be made. Either way, Longarm would be satisfied.

Leaving the vest behind, hoping the rifleman would believe he had the lawman spotted, Longarm crawled beneath his decoy and scrambled up the hillside in the protection of the shallow wash.

He reached the end of the wash about thirty yards below the top of the slope. For the past twenty yards or more he had been belly down to the ground as the runnel line petered

out. If the rifleman had not changed position since Longarm
last spotted him—unlikely but possible—he would be fifty
or so yards to Longarm's left and somewhat below him on
the hillside.

That was a big "if."

Longarm drew his Colt, took a deep breath, and bellied
forward.

The slope where the rifleman had been was empty except
for grass and a few scattered spears of soapweed. The man
had moved somewhere, and...

Movement flickered at the periphery of Longarm's vision. While Longarm had been crawling up the wash, the
rifleman had been moving across the slope to reach it also.
He was at least forty yards below Longarm, with his attention still down toward the decoy vest. His back was to
Longarm, the rifle muzzle and stock visible in a ready position.

Proper procedure would be to inform the gentleman that
he was under arrest and ask him to put his weapon down
and surrender himself to the judgement of the law.

*Proper procedure. You bet,* Longarm thought.

Forty yards was a hell of a long pistol shot, but spitting
distance for whatever rifle the assassin was carrying. Asking
the murderer to surrender would be a backhanded form of
suicide, and Longarm knew it.

He rolled over and came up into a sitting position, braced
his arms on his knees with both hands steadying the heavy
Colt .44, took careful aim, and touched her off.

The heavy, soft lead slug took the man just under his
left shoulder blade, a good eight inches off the mark Longarm had taken at the base of his spine, but still a fine shot
at the distance, He sagged forward. Longarm could hear a
cough-like rush of breath being expelled from him at the
impact.

He went to his knees, and Longarm fired twice more.
He reloaded the Colt before he walked down the hill, hoping
but not really expecting that the rifleman would still be alive
to answer some questions.

The expectation turned out to be more accurate than the hope had been.

Walter Randolph's eyes were glazed and lifeless when Longarm rolled him over.

"I sure wish you and me could have a talk," Longarm told the dead man. "I know damn good and well you weren't hired by any buckskin horse to go around shooting people. The question is, were you after me because of that horse, or something to do with those government hunters? Or were you just scared I was onto you about those wants on you from down New Mexico way?" He shook his head.

This was one of those times when he fervently wished that dead men could tell tales.

# Chapter 13

"That rifle and the cartridges that fit it tell the tale," Billy Vail said.

It was only two hours by passenger coach to Denver, which was a luxury Longarm's work rarely afforded. He had brought in Walter Randolph's body and the oddly made rifle the man had been carrying. The rifle was topped with a steel tube nearly as long as the barrel with a set of precisely adjustable crosshair sights inside the tube. It was an unusual but most effective tool for a professional assassin.

"I sent the bullet taken from Wolfe's body to the Justice Department for examination. They weren't sure but they said they thought it came from a French Lebel rifle." He pointed toward the ugly but efficient firearm. "That thing right there says the man who shot at you is the same fellow who pulled the trigger on Charles Wolfe."

Longarm rubbed the back of his neck and sighed. He was getting a headache. "That's nice to know, but it sure doesn't close the case for us."

Vail nodded grimly. "Makes it more complicated, if anything. We won't be asking Mr. Randolph any questions about who hired him. Or why."

"We know one thing," Longarm said. "It wasn't any damned horse that paid his fees."

"A hundred dollars a shooting is what the grapevine says he charged," Vail said.

"Which means someone was feeling powerful well threatened," Longarm completed the thought. "I just wish some of this—any of it—made some kind of sense to me. Two government hunters, one certainly and the other presumably shot by Randolph while they were trying to track down one outlaw horse."

"And one deputy marshal assaulted from ambush by the same man, with the same object in mind, and apparently for the same reasons."

"Apparently but not absolutely certainly. I'd faced him once without knowing who he was. It's still possible he thought I was after him because of the outstanding wants with his name on them."

Billy shook his head. "Too much coincidence there. You did tell me you had made a point of telling people you were after the buckskin. Both hunters were known to be after the horse. It only stands to reason."

Longarm shrugged. "One way or another, Billy, we're going to know the answers before we call it quits on this thing."

"Technically speaking, the Interior Department's request has been filled. You did apprehend, so to speak, the murderer of their hunters."

"You know as well as I do, Billy, that Walter Randolph was a professional at his game. He wasn't the type who shot people for the thrill of it. Nor for pleasure or personal grievances. The grapevine's pretty clear about that too. He shot for money. Period. Somebody paid him to go after those hunters and probably paid him to go after me. He didn't stay in business as long as he did by shooting every lawman who had a want on him. Run away, sure. Which is what I think he did down in Monument the other day. Or shoot back in self-defense if somebody was on his trail. But to track me like that and set up an ambush? I think that says he was hired for the job. Hell, Billy, he could have ridden off for Kansas or back into the mountains, and I'd never have had a clue which way to run him. He would have known that.

"So if we tried to write this one off as closed, the guy with the money will just find another gunman to do his work. Lord knows there are enough he can choose from, at any level of ability, from a ten-dollar muscle boy on up." Longarm made a face and pulled a cheroot from his pocket.

"You're saying you want to stay with it, then?"

"I'm saying we haven't done the job yet. I'll do whatever you tell me to, of course, but unless you have some reason to let people go on shooting down government hunters, or for letting that buckskin stud alone, then, yes, I think I should stay on it. Quitting in the middle of the job would leave me with a sour taste in my mouth, Billy. Might even ruin the flavor of good rye."

Vail smiled. "I couldn't let that happen, could I?"

"All right, then. I'll stop over at my room and get a change of clothing. I'll take the next southbound cars and get back to business."

"Hi." He said it without much spirit, dropped his hat onto the empty chair beside him, and accepted the cup of coffee and slice of pie Birgita set before him.

"You sound awfully low today."

"I would have to admit to it, pretty lady." He forced a smile. "I don't suppose you've been bothered by any dragons lately that I could slay for you. Something positive would sure make me feel better about now."

109

Birgita glanced around the restaurant, saw that no one seemed to need her attention for the moment, and dropped into a chair across the table. "What's wrong, Custis?"

"Oh, lots of questions. No answers. It happens all the time. I—uh—don't suppose you know anything about Walter Randolph's friends." He grimaced. "No one else does around here, that's for sure."

For a moment the girl looked blank. Then she made the connection. "You mean Randy."

"Yeah. Walter, really, despite what he'd been called around here."

She shook her head. "I can't remember anyone in particular that he was seen with. I mean, he would speak to people and all that. But I can't think of any particular friends." She looked thoughtful. "There was one man. . . ." She shook her head. "I'm really not sure I can remember."

"Try," Longarm urged. The coffee was good, but the pie crust was soggy. He shoved the plate away with the pie half eaten.

"Tom? That might have been the name. They ate together in here once or twice. That was before Randy . . . I mean Walter . . . started giving me trouble, so I wasn't paying any particular attention to him. He was just another customer. And I'm not very good at names." She smiled. "Except yours, of course. I won't forget yours, Custis."

"Do you remember anything about this Tom?" he asked her.

Birgita shook her head. "I'm not even sure of the name, Custis. He was just another cowboy. They all have that same look about them, as far as I can tell. Sun-dried and needing a bath. I really couldn't tell you anything about him."

"Thanks for trying, anyway," he said. He tried to make it sound as if he meant it, but the truth was that she had not given him any information of value. A cowboy would not have the kind of money it would take to hire a precision rifle specialist like Walter Randolph. Not at thirty dollars a month, he wouldn't.

Longarm finished his coffee and laid a coin on the table.

"Will you be staying in town overnight?" She asked it softly, and there was no mistaking her meaning.

"I expect I will be."

"I—uh—I'd feel safer if there was someone to walk me home after work."

Longarm smiled. "That's what I'm paid for, ma'am—to protect and serve the public."

"Nine o'clock, then?"

"I won't forget."

He left, but even the anticipation of the evening to come was not enough to dispel the gloom he was feeling. Every direction he turned seemed to lead to just another dead end.

# Chapter 14

The telegraph operator found him at breakfast and interrupted what until then had been a satisfying meal.

"Marshal Long?" The thin, spectacled young man glanced
at the message sheet in his hand and asked again, "Custis
Long?"

"You found the right party."

"This just came in. I thought you ought to know about
it right away." He handed the flimsy sheet to Longarm,
touched his cap, and was hurrying back to his untended key
before Longarm even had a chance to thank him.

The wire was from Billy Vail, and it brought a few pithy
cuss words to Longarm's lips.

EL PASO COUNTY RANCHER HORACE PRIT-
KIN REPORTED KILLED BY ROGUE BUCKSKIN

BEFORE DAWN YESTERDAY STOP YOUR
JUDGMENT QUERY

It was signed by Billy Vail.

Either Justice or Interior had been informed of the death,
Longarm figured, so there would be local officers already
involved or the message would not have been passed. Still,
he wanted to see if there was anything he could learn,
wherever the damned ranch was. He could answer Billy's
question later, when he knew more about it. He paid for
his meal and went to reclaim his horse and get directions
to the Pritkin place.

The ranch turned out to be a hardscrabble outfit half a
day's ride to the east, out onto the hot, dry plains. The
travel did nothing to improve Longarm's frustrated mood.

He found the right place after two wrong guesses from
the poor directions he had been given, but as soon as he
arrived he knew he should have known better both other
times. The yard of the Pritkin place was filled with wagons
and light rigs and a grouping of saddle horses. He tied his
mount with the other and went to the door. A thin-faced,
tired-looking woman in her middle years answered his knock.

Longarm removed his hat. "I'm looking for a Mrs. Pritkin, ma'am."

"Are you a friend of Horace?"

"No, ma'am, I'm a deputy United States marshal. I've
been asked to look into the matter of a rogue horse down
this way."

The woman's face twisted. "I wish you had been here
sooner, Marshal."

"Yes, ma'am."

A pair of small girls, one still a toddler and the other
reaching no higher than her mother's waist, ran to the hag-
gard woman and grabbed at her skirts. They buried their
faces in the material and peeped up at Longarm one eye at
a time.

"Are you . . . ?"

"Yes, Marshal, I am Louise Pritkin, the . . ." Her face

113

twisted again. "The widow of Mr. Pritkin," she finished.

"I'm sorry to bother you at a time like this, ma'am."

She nodded her understanding. "It's all right. Come inside, please."

Longarm thanked her, knocked his boots free of dirt, and entered the house. He also gave Mrs. Pritkin a second, closer look after seeing the ages of the two children, and revised his guess of the widow's age downward by a good many years. The country could be hard on a woman, and most aged long before their time out here.

The inside of the house was crowded and noisy. Neighbors had obviously come from miles around, bearing platters and crocks of foodstuffs that were piled high on a table that dominated the main room of the sod house. The ladies sat in every available seat while the children played loudly in the corners. There were few men in evidence, and Longarm guessed that they would be gathered in the barn to talk and drink cheap liquor from crockery jars. Even without the men, though, the room was crowded.

At the moment, of course, the focal point of the room was the body of Horace Pritkin.

A sheet had been draped under his body, but it was still easy to see that a door had been taken from somewhere and laid between two chairs to make the platform. The men were probably engaged in the work of constructing a coffin, Longarm thought.

The dead man had been washed and dressed in his best clothing, and some unsteady hand had done a poor job of shaving what was visible of his face. The entire left side of the man's head was swathed in linen bandages, covering the massive damage a striking hoof had done.

Pritkin had been dead little more than a day, but in this heat the burial would have to be held soon. They would probably put him into the ground this afternoon. For the moment, at least, the odor in the room was of food and soap, but that could not be expected to last.

Longarm stood beside the body for a moment with his hat in his hands and his eyes cast down, paying his respects to a man he had never met. Then he turned away. Mrs. Pritkin was still beside him.

"Could I offer you something to eat, Marshal?"

His first inclination was to refuse. He did not want to cause the woman any trouble. She had more than enough of that already, with her husband dead and two children to raise. But almost as quickly he realized that there can be a form of relief in activity, too, when the world has turned to a dark and empty place. It might be more of a kindness to accept than to refuse.

"That's kind of you, ma'am. I'd be grateful."

She slipped away to the table and busied herself with fixing him a plate of rolls and fried meats and dishes of the kind that could be carried long distances and served cold. She returned and handed him the loaded plate. "I suppose you want to ask me some things, or you wouldn't have come."

"Yes, ma'am. Thank you."

"We could talk in the bedroom there. Bring your plate along. It's all right."

"If you're sure."

"It's all right. Really."

He followed her into the small room she had shared with her husband.

Horace Pritkin obviously had not been a prosperous man —not yet—but he had been a worker, and Longarm suspected he would also have been the kind to work until he did prosper. The house, although built of sod, was solidly made, and much larger than most soddies. Most were single-room affairs barely large enough to accommodate a table, a stove, and few beds. Pritkin had built the main room plus a bedroom and a lean-to kitchen. The doors and windows were framed with carefully worked wood, and a craftsman's touch showed in the furniture as well. Longarm thought he might very well have liked Pritkin, had they ever met.

There was a small dressing table in the bedroom, but the chair that should have sat before it was missing and was probably in use in the main room where the guests had

115

gathered. Longarm had no choice but to perch on the side of the bed with his plate in his hand and a weight of discomfort on his shoulders. He felt awkward among the mourners who had known the dead man.

"Are you all right, Marshal?" Mrs. Pritkin looked concerned, and Longarm felt a flicker of embarrassment that at a moment like this it should be she who was trying to assure his comfort when it so clearly should have been the other way around.

"Yes, ma'am, I'm fine, but...I have to ask you about your husband, ma'am. I'm sorry, but..."

"It is quite all right." She sighed and looked away. After a time she said, "Mr. Pritkin was a good man, Marshal. Oh, I know that's an easy thing to say about the dead, but in Mr. Pritkin's case it was true. He really was a very good man. A good provider and always gentle with his children. I never saw him strike out in anger at any person or any thing, Marshal, not even our old mule." A hint of a smile tugged at the corners of her mouth, and Longarm guessed that there were some fond and funny stories to be told there. Someday, he hoped, she would be able to remember and relate those stories without pain.

"Mr. Pritkin's dream had always been to be a husbandman. A raiser of livestock and not just a tiller of the soil. We had a fair farm back in Ohio, but Mr. Pritkin had a large heart and large dreams, and he wanted a land and an opportunity large enough to match them. We came here three years ago with seed and tools and a little money from the sale of our farm. Our smallest was not born then. She came to us afterward."

Longarm nodded and refrained from asking any questions. It was a thing she would do better to tell in her own way.

"We filed on our land, and Mr. Pritkin purchased ten heifers carrying their first calves. Ten head. It seemed like so very many at the time, compared with the farming we had known in the East."

Again Longarm nodded. A family with three milk cows

116

had been prosperous indeed in the West Virginia of his youth.

"We lost one of the heifers and her calf the first winter, but the others calved successfully." She sighed. "Mr. Pritkin was proud of the increase. This year he would have sold the first of the steers from that increase. It would have been his first success as a grower of livestock. We had to depend on cropping and gardening to carry us through until then."

Her face twisted again, and Longarm thought she was going to weep, but she managed to control herself.

"Of course, he never got to realize that dream, did he? He never will."

"No, ma'am."

She gave him a strained expression that must have been intended as a smile. "I shouldn't rattle on at you like this."

"It's fine, ma'am. I'm in no hurry."

"Yes, well, about yesterday morning." She looked vaguely surprised for a moment. "Has it been that short a time? I suppose it has at that."

Longarm waited for her to continue when she was ready.

"Some time before dawn yesterday—" she reached out absently and stroked the feather pillow that must have been her husband's—"we heard the cattle begin to bawl. It woke both of us. Mr. Pritkin got out of bed in the dark. Little Nellie, she's the youngest, had been bothered by something in the night and had come in to slip in between us, so Mr. Pritkin did not light the lamp. I'm sure he did not want to disturb her sleep." A flow of quiet tears had begun to slide down the woman's work-worn cheeks.

"He said something about the windmill. The cattle usually do not bawl at night, but I remember they became thirsty and very agitated once when the windmill failed and there was no water in the tank for them. Mr. Pritkin was going out to see if he could fix whatever was wrong."

The tears were coming freely now, and her shoulders were heaving. "He never even got dressed, never put his shoes on. He went out on that hard soil barefoot and died with mud on his feet. He would have hated that. He would

117

much rather have died with boots on his feet, and spurs, like a cowman. I wish..."

She was crying too hard to go on now. Longarm leaned forward and patted her on the shoulder, but there was nothing he could do that would help. It was much too late for that now. He set his untouched plate of food aside—he was no longer the slightest bit hungry—and went out into the other room to see if he could find one of the women to go in and comfort the grieving widow.

With a sense of frustration lying heavy on him, Longarm went back outside and around to the barn where he could expect to find the menfolk.

There were eight or ten of them there. They had cleared a space and were using Pritkin's tools to build a coffin. Several jugs and at least half a dozen bottles were in evidence nearby.

"Who're you?" one of them asked.

Longarm introduced himself.

"You're too damn late to do anything about it," another man accused.

"True, but I'd like to find out anything you men might know. I couldn't prevent this death, but there might be another if nothing gets done here."

The man grunted. "What do you want to know?"

"Are you sure it was a horse that killed him?"

"Hell, yes. It was a horse. You can see the mark of the shoe plain as pitch. Hit him high on the side of the head. The mark's clear enough, but I suppose you'll have to unwrap the poor man's head in front of his woman just so's you can be satisfied your own self."

"I can take your word for it," Longarm said softly. The man was obviously upset and must have been a good friend of Horace Pritkin. "I expect you know what you saw."

"Damn right I do."

"How do you know it was the buckskin that killed him?"

The man sneered. "Fat lot about horses you seem to know, *Marshal.*" He made the title sound like a cussword. "There's damn few horses that will strike a man and prac-

118

tically none that will do it deliberate. A man gets throwed, a horse will go half crazy an' turn himself inside out tryin' to keep from stepping on the poor devil."

Longarm nodded. That was hardly news to him, but he was not going to tell the aggrieved and proddy rancher that he already knew that and perhaps just a bit more about horseflesh.

"So, to begin with, it just ain't possible that there could be two horses in the area that would strike a man down. It would have to be the buckskin on account of that alone. But more'n that, we know it's so because a good cow and three two-year-old steers was cut away from the bunch and drove off by that horse. Four head taken off to who knows where by that devilish son of a bitch. And you nor nobody else can tell me there's two horses in the county that would do *both* those things."

Mrs. Pritkin had broken down before she had told him that. Or perhaps she did not even know it yet, Longarm thought. With all her other troubles, her neighbors might well be avoiding giving her that news, since it would mean a heavy loss of income for her and her two children. A family in this stage of the long, hard struggle to make a go of life on homesteaded land could not afford the loss of four animals from their herd, whether Mrs. Pritkin chose to stay and try to run the place herself or chose instead to sell.

"You know the herd that well?" Longarm found himself asking.

"Damn straight, I do." The man sounded belligerent and ready to start a fight over that or any other slight, real or imagined. "I'm their closest neighbor, and Horace and me worked side by side day in an' day out. We always pitched together. Helped the man spud in his well an' he helped me with mine. Cut and laid up sod together and everything since then. We come in on the same train together and took to one another right off. That Horace, he was as good a man as I'll ever know in this life." He glared at Longarm, inviting him to disagree and at the same time making it clear that in his opinion the lawman was not and never would be the equal of homesteader Horace Pritkin.

"There's tracks clear enough," another man put in, "where the horse was shifting and cutting. You can see it yourself, if you want."

"Not any more," another of the men corrected. "The cows an' our horses, we've pretty much trompled what tracks there was." To Longarm he said, "You can check with Deputy Sheriff Mackey. He was here yesterday before everything got trampled over."

Longarm nodded his thanks. "Did anyone see the buckskin, though? Mrs. Pritkin, maybe?"

The closest neighbor squinted and thought about that for a moment. He seemed somewhat calmer now. "She'd have told me if she'd seen the horse. She said she heard the cattle bawling an' then Horace went outside. Said she heard a horse tramping around out there but she figured it was one of their own. When Horace didn't come back after a while she got up to light the fire an' get breakfast on. Said when he still didn't come an' the biscuits had been cooking long enough that she knew he'd be ready for some, she went out to call him. Thought he was out there workin' on the windmill. Instead he was lyin' out there dead with his head caved in." Emotion gripped the man and he turned away so it would not be seen by his neighbors.

*The Pritkins had at least one damned good neighbor,* Longarm thought.

"I appreciate your help," Longarm told them.

He turned away, feeling very much out of place. It was a long ride back to town, too far for him to make it now before nightfall, and he was hungry. But he did not want to intrude any further on these people. He had learned about all he could expect to here, little though it was. Pritkin had indeed been killed by a horse even though, as usual, no one had actually seen the horse. Still, the neighbor had been right. There could not be another man-killer who would also cut a herd of cattle and take them away.

Longarm fired up a cheroot to help quiet the rumblings in his stomach and retrieved his horse from the group tied

120

to Pritkin's stoutly constructed corral rails. He mounted and rode out past the windmill, knowing in advance that he would not be able to follow the tracks the cattle had left leading dimly eastward from the homestead, but unwilling to quit until he was beaten by the hard earth and the dry, lifeless grass.

# Chapter 15

Longarm yawned and pulled his sandwiched blanket and yellow oilskin slicker closer around his shoulders. It had been a bad night, from one end to the other.

His abortive swing eastward on the dim trail of the missing cattle had been just about as useful as he had expected. The faint and quite possibly false trail was visible for little better than a mile. It could as easily have been left by undriven cattle coming in to the water as by the missing animals. That slow detour, though, and the hour of his start had absolutely guaranteed that he could not make it back to the comforts of a bed at any reasonable hour, so he had had to make a dry camp in a cluster of rocks below a small, steep-walled mesa.

Worse, by the time he realized he would have to stop, and without water at that, he was in a stretch of the rolling, hilly terrain that offered no wood for a fire. By the time he realized that, it was too dark even to search for cow chips that he could have burned. If he had had a light he could have found more than enough fuel for a fire, but if he had a light that would mean that he had wood to make it and would not need the chips. Altogether, it was a lousy situation that left him chilled and coffeeless.

Supper had been a few lint-speckled strips of jerked beef from his saddlebags and a few swallows from the bottle of Maryland rye he carried. Breakfast would be more of the same.

Longarm stretched and wondered why the morning felt so far advanced when the light was still so weak. Then, thinking about it for the first time since he woke up, he looked overhead and the reason became clear. It should already have been light, but some time before dawn a battalion of thunderheads had moved in above him. A line of weather was making, and Longarm knew as well as the next man how fierce a plains storm could become. It was not impossible to ride through one—far from it—but it was damned miserable.

It was, he thought, just what he needed to cap off a perfect night. No fire, no coffee, and now he was about to be soaking wet.

*All you need, boy,* he told himself, *is a toothache.* He wondered briefly how Billy Vail would react to a retirement request. After all, it wasn't as if he were accomplishing anything, the way things were going lately. At this rate he would not be cheating the taxpayers any the worse if he hung it up and gorged at the public trough for the rest of his days.

*Feelin' sorry for yourself this morning, ain't you, boy?* he asked himself.

He stood and repacked his gear, which took only a moment, and saddled his horse. The yellow slicker he draped over the top of his bedroll, tying it separately instead of

123

wrapping it around the sausage-shaped roll. When that rain started he would need it more than his blanket did.

He checked his horse's feet for impacted stones or mud, a habit of long standing, a swung aboard in the dim, gray light of a belated dawn. The air smelled fresh and clean and full of rain.

"Come on, stupid, let's get down the road," he mumbled aloud. The horse responded readily enough to his heel pressure, and Longarm reached back to search in his saddlebag for that jerky and remaining Maryland rye. If he had to be uncomfortable he might just as well minimize it.

The storm hit a half hour or so later.

The sky had closed down dark and forbidding until it was no more bright or inviting than a January twilight in a mining camp, and Longarm felt as if the entire weight of the sky was pressing down against his lungs. Breath came hard in the moist, heavy atmosphere, and Longarm found himself wanting to stab the horse into a run in an effort to escape the coming storm, even though he knew full well that he had noplace to run to.

A pale tan slash across the parched, grassy surface of the land turned out to be a deep, vertically walled wash with twists and turns that offered the seductive lure of a break from the wind that was beginning to rise out of the northwest. But Longarm knew that hiding in a dry wash during a rainstorm was just about as bright as lighting your way with a match in a powder magazine. Even so, he looked down into the wash with wistful regret as he skirted the edge and rode around it. In a matter of minutes that wash could be full of running water, but at the moment it looked secure and inviting.

The wind was picking up in cold, hard gusts now, and Longarm tugged his Stetson down tighter on his head. He turned the collar of his coat up and buttoned it to the throat.

Wind was one thing, but these playful gusts were coming from any and every direction. One would hit him full in the face with awesome force approaching fury. A second or two and there would be no wind at all, just a dead forbidding calm. Then another blast would come from another direction hard enough to stagger the horse and send Longarm swaying in his saddle.

The horse liked it no better than Longarm did. The animal jogged ahead with its head sullenly low and its ears pinned back with displeasure.

"I know, old crock, but there's nothing we can do about it." Longarm would have traded his next month's pay— well, a week's pay, anyhow—for the use of a barn right then. For the use of one small, unimproved snake-den of a cave. Anything, even a tree to hide behind.

The rain followed on the brisk, snapping heels of the wind.

He could see it a mile before it reached him: a solid gray wall of falling water that raced down on him from the northwest with the speed of a fast freight on a downhill run.

He could hear it when it was still a quarter of a mile distant. A soft, steady roar not unlike the sound of a waterfall or a particularly vicious rapids when heard from far away. It came nearer with a hiss that rose in volume and intensity until it reached and quickly overwhelmed him.

The rain, huge droplets even on the outer fringe of the storm wall, hit with the coldly merciless chill of hail against his wind-dried skin. There was no hail, but the cold and the size of the drops made Longarm look to see, convinced at that first moment that he was being pelted by tiny balls of ice instead of water.

At first he could feel each striking droplet as an individual sensation, but within seconds his clothes were drenched. He had been so interested in watching the approach of the storm that he had completely forgotten to pull his slicker from behind his cantle.

Now, he thought ruefully, it was too damned late. He could not do more than trap the rain and turn his slicker into a portable steamroom if he put the protection on over sopping wet clothes. Better, he decided, to leave the slicker where it was, so it could protect his bedroll. He hunched

125

his shoulders and allowed the fretful horse to drop from a jog back into a slow, stolid walk, plodding one foot at a time through the harsh battering of the rain.

The storm lashed at the sun-browned grasses. The wind returned soon after the passage of the rain wall and contributed its share to the destruction of the grass.

An Easterner living on the soft, pearly loam of a farm would have rejoiced at the rainfall and expected it to give new life to the grass. Longarm knew better. Here the storm would batter and destroy, but the hard-baked earth was capable of accepting practically none of the moisture. Instead of sinking into the ground, the water sheeted and raced across it, gouging the washes ever deeper and tearing at the roots of the meager forage that covered the plains.

Longarm rode slowly through the fury, chilled to the bone but accepting the inevitability of the discomfort because there were no other options.

He reined the horse around the smallest puddles when he could see no grass stems to assure him that there was solid earth beneath the mud-brown surface of the rain-churned water. This was no time to ride his horse into a prairie dog town and snap a leg out of laziness. So he zigzagged back and forth across the solid flow of moving water that the earth had become, slowing his progress all the more.

In a matter of minutes the hard, dry footing had become treacherous. The driving rain turned the ground into a grease-slick expanse of mud on top of an almost ceramic-hard base. It was fully as bad as walking a horse on ice. A single misstep could lead to an ugly fall. A slow walk was all that prudence would allow.

After ten minutes or so, Longarm raised his head. He cocked his head to the side and squinted into the force of the rain. Drops striking the edge of his hatbrim splattered and drove a stinging spray into his eyes and down his cheeks in spite of the protection offered by the hat.

Longarm threw his head back and looked almost straight up. He could see the rain like pale threads hurtling down from the steel-gray sky.

"Horse," he said out loud, "I think we have found the perfect day for a man to contemplate his own humility." He began to grin. Another moment and he was laughing loud and hard into the teeth of the storm. He was so damned miserable that it was funny. The horse flicked its ears and turned its nose toward his right stirrup to sneak a look at its rider.

"Get along, you old snide," Longarm said cheerfully. "I think I know where we're going, unless I'm mistaken about that notched bluff line over there. Get along, stupid."

Longarm removed his hat, and a sheet of rainwater cascaded off the brim to the wooden stoop set in front of the door. "Ma'am? Sorry to disturb you, but . . ." He motioned toward the still-intense storm at his back.

"You look cheerful for such an unpleasant day, Marshal."

He grinned. "Reckon I thought of it that way myself till I realized I couldn't get no wetter nor no more miserable than I already was. For some reason, that got me into a good humor. Which I will admit is the first of those I have experienced in some little time now."

She looked puzzled, but she did not question him about it. "Do come in, Marshal."

"If you're sure it wouldn't be a bother, ma'am. I could hide out in the shed just as easy. If you'd be more comfortable that way."

"Not at all. Come in, please." She stepped out of the doorway, and Longarm followed her inside.

The inside of the house was as he remembered it, although outdoors now there was no sign of her free-roaming chickens nor of the hogs in their sty. The animals knew enough to come in out of the rain even if a deputy U. S. marshal did not.

"Would you care for a cup of tea, Marshal?"

"That would be real kind of you, Mrs. Crowder."

She looked him over with a critical eye and then shook her head. "Actually, Marshal, you look like the rats sailors dredge out of their bilges at the end of a long voyage and

127

throw out into the harbor waters. Disheveled and quite thoroughly wet. I could offer you a glass of something stronger, if you would prefer."

"Stronger, ma'am?" He was having delightful visions all of a sudden of Maryland rye. It was improbable, of course, but stranger things had happened.

"I have some brandy, Marshal."

So much for that dream. He smiled. "Medicinal, ma'am?"

"As a matter of fact, I keep some on hand for the enjoyment of drinking it. The old saw about using it for medicinal purposes is a sham, and frankly I have no use for shams in my life. To answer your question, I simply enjoy it."

"If you don't mind then, ma'am, I will consider myself put into my place. And, yes, I would very much enjoy a glass of your brandy."

She gave him that critical observation again and sighed. Longarm got the impression that Mrs. Crowder had just shrugged her shoulders with resignation, even though he had not seen her physically move a single muscle. "You really do look terrible, Marshal. Cold?"

He nodded.

"I thought as much. All right. Step behind that blanket over there. Strip off those wet things and wrap youself in the blanket. There is one folded at the foot of the bed. You can cover yourself with that while I dry your clothes by the stove."

"You don't have to . . ."

"Nonsense. Of course I have to. It is a matter of perspective and self-respect. If a stray dog comes to my door wet and cold, I bring him in to towel him dry and let him sleep by the fire until he can go on about his business. I have done as much often enough. How can I do that and consider myself a charitable human being if I am not willing to do as much for a person, Marshal Long?" She looked at him. "Now please go on and do as I asked. I will get the brandy while you are changing."

Longarm thought he might actually have understood what

she had said, and he wondered for a moment if that should bother him.

Remembering her prejudices from the last time he had been here, he removed his gunbelt first and hung it by the door, then stepped behind the hanging screen to strip his clothes off down to the drawers. He stopped there for a second, not really wanting to be so completely naked with Mrs. Crowder near, but the lightweight cloth was plastered to him as thoroughly as if he had just come from a swim in a creek. He pulled them off.

The blanket was more than large enough to cover him from throat to ankle, but he felt like a wooden Indian with it draped tight and clutched at chest and belly with both hands. That feeling was not improved when he stepped out into the room with Mrs. Crowder.

She took one look at him and began to laugh. "If you could see yourself, Marshal—If your colleagues could see you now—"

Longarm found himself beginning to grin. "Worse yet," he said, "if one of those old boys with wants on their heads could see me now, why, I'd never be able to arrest another one of 'em, I bet." He was laughing now, feeling more at ease.

"I daresay you are correct, at that," she said with a chuckle. She pointed. "Your glass is on the table."

"Thanks."

There were two glasses poured, he noticed, and the woman had poured a full measure for herself as well as for her guest.

The brandy left a fiery trail down his throat and spread with satisfying warmth into his belly. Since getting out of the weather, he had almost forgotten how cold the rain had been. "Thanks," he said again, this time with much more feeling.

Mrs. Crowder looked thoughtful. "You know, Marshal, you came here seeking to do injury to an innocent animal. I reacted badly to that thought. It had not occurred to me what your duties must be at other times, on other assignments. Not all of your opponents are innocent, are they?"

"No, ma'am, this would have to be the exception. And I'm not so sure as you are that it is an exception." He told her about Horace Pritkin and what the dead man's family was like. "They're good folks," he concluded. "They didn't deserve the troubles they've been given."

"No, I suppose not. Nor do any of us."

"No, ma'am." After a moment he said, "Mrs. Crowder, one way or another, this business with your friend Buck has got to stop. It would be a favor to a lot of folks if you would help me. You might have some ideas about where..."

She cut him off. "I won't interfere with your duties, Marshal. But I will not assist you in the destruction of a truly noble animal like Bucky, either. No matter what your plea or how noble your aims, I could not do that. Please don't ask me again."

"I won't, ma'am. That's a promise."

"I shall hold you to it."

"Yes, ma'am." He took another drink of the brandy, and this time he did not even wish that it was Maryland rye instead.

# Chapter 16

Longarm awakened feeling far, far better than he had the previous morning. He was stretched out on a mound of hay in Mrs. Crowder's shed, and the early morning light was bright in the clear, clean blue of the sky. The Front Range mountains stood out in sharp relief against the western skyline and looked close enough to hit with a pebble from a slungshot.

He took his time about getting his Colt into just the right position, finished dressing quickly, and visited the outhouse. By that time he could smell breakfast cooking, and he was more than ready for it.

Immediately afterward, he said his goodbyes and got back on the road. Mrs. Crowder had been much more hospitable this time, but he had work to do and no reason for staying.

"I will not wish you luck in this job, Marshal," she said as a last parting shot.

"No, ma'am, but I sure do thank you for your kindness." He tipped his hat to her and reined the horse away.

The sun was well up by that time, and the still-damp plains were steaming. Puddles of mud and gray-brown water stood in the depressions, and the hard clay soil was still moistly greasy in places.

Longarm found himself wishing that the buckskin would strike again that morning. At least there would be tracks to follow if it did, and he could use the break.

Something, possibly moisture lingering in the air, seemed to magnify the sun, and after a time Longarm stripped off his coat and turned to strap it on top of his slicker.

BEEEEYYANGGG-G-G-G!

The shot came from somewhere off to his left, ricocheted off the ground, and whined away into the distance.

Longarm's reaction was instantaneous. He yanked the Winchester from its boot beneath his right leg and spurred the horse into a jump as another shot sought him out, passing somewhere behind him as the horse leaped.

Longarm flattened himself against the neck of the running horse and glanced to his left.

There were two of them, afoot in a shallow depression. Each man had a rifle in his hand, and the one on the right was taking aim for a third attempt. Longarm saw the rifle barrel steady. He drew back on his reins slightly to check the speed of the horse. He saw the muzzle jump and the faint puff of white smoke issue from the barrel. The shot passed harmlessly in front of him.

Enough was enough, though. Give a man sufficient chances and he was bound to get lucky eventually.

Longarm cut his horse hard to the right and took him over one of the endless rises that formed this part of the plains country.

The gunmen would expect him to keep going hard and fast, he reasoned. But leaving an ambusher behind and able to try again had never been Longarm's idea of wisdom. He

132

held the horse in a belly-down circling run around in a wide sweep that should keep him out of sight from the two riflemen and bring him up behind them. Whoever they were, they had to have reached the spot by horseback, and those horses could not be too far away. The question was whether Longarm could get to the horses first.

He spotted the animals after a few minutes. They had been left at the bottom of a deep wash with crumbling sides and a muddy quagmire for a bottom. The riflemen were not yet in sight. They had chosen to leave their horses far from their shooting stand so they would be undiscovered.

That much of their plan had worked, but now it was going to backfire on them.

Longarm leaned back in his saddle and forced his horse into a rump-sliding descent into the wash downstream from where the ambushers had left their mounts.

There was nothing to tie the horse to and Longarm put little faith into a ground-tie unless he had no other choice. He dropped the reins and placed a melon-sized clod of hard clay on top of them to give a little resistance if the horse tried to move. Then, with the Winchester in his hand and the double-action Colt ready at his waist, he began to follow the twisting gully bottom toward where he had seen the waiting horses.

He moved slowly and with care, inching his way forward with the Winchester cocked and held at the ready, keeping hard against the gully wall. His ears were tuned even more keenly than his eyes, because in a situation like this he was much more likely to hear the enemy than see him for the first contact. And with two men to face, that first contact was all-important.

He heard the horses first, heard the suck and plop of hooves being lifted and replaced in the soft mud of the wash bottom, heard one of them blow and stamp with a wet, mushy sound. There was a slow series of soft plopping noises, and a moment later he could smell the sharp odor of fresh manure. He was very close to them indeed, but a turn in the fall of the wash hid him from sight.

Just to make sure, Longarm eased forward until he could see the horses' rumps. There was no sign of the ambushers who had ridden them here. Longarm leaned back into the protection of the curving wall and waited.

The sun was high enough now to reach past the wall rim overhead, and the heat in such close quarters turned the gully into a Turkish bath. Sweat formed under the brim of Longarm's hat and rolled down his face. He wiped it away and smoothed the shape of his swooping mustache where he had disturbed it. He leaned up against the moist clay of the gully wall and waited with the unruffled patience of a hunter.

After a time—it could have been five minutes or fifteen—he could hear footsteps on the firmer ground above the rim of the wash.

There was a low grunt of exertion and the sound of dirt clods skittering down the wall into the mud below.

*Looks like you have company,* Longarm told himself.

From the sounds the men were only a few paces away, so he transferred the Winchester to his left hand and slid the heavy .44 into his fist. At close range, speed was almost as important as accuracy, and the revolver would be as accurate as was necessary but much quicker.

"I tell you I think . . ."

"I don't care what you think, damn it. The point is, the bastard got away."

"Aw, we'll get another chance at him."

"We better," the other voice said accusingly.

Longarm wondered if he might learn something of interest—like why in hell they were shooting at him—if he kept still a little longer. But he could hear the thin rattle of rein chains and the sharp slap of a cinch strap being yanked tight. It seemed that his friends were leaving.

Longarm took a step forward. "You have another chance," he informed them.

The two men stood with gaping jaws, shocked into immobility for an instant.

"Reckon you boys are under arrest," Longarm drawled.

"Assault on a Federal officer, attempted murder, and I might be able to think of a few more if I put my mind to it."

Both men stood with their rifles in their hands but with their revolvers holstered and as good as useless, while Longarm had his Colt already in hand. As far as Longarm was concerned, the arrest was as good as made, and he was glad. He wanted a chance to talk to these two birds and find out what they were up to.

Neither of the ambushers was a particularly impressive specimen of manhood. They were dressed in range clothing, but looked much seedier and shabbier than regular cowhands. Most of that breed paid an inordinate amount of attention to their hats and boots in particular, while these two wore grimy, shapeless hats and rundown boots. They looked, Longarm thought, like they were in need of drinking money, which could well explain what they had been doing with those rifles in their inexpert hands.

One stood eight or ten feet in front of Longarm, while the second man was beyond both horses and probably twenty feet away.

"Drop the guns, boys, and we'll go for a ride. No need to get excited and no need for you to die. You'll have plenty of time in the future to repent your sins and change your ways." He gave them a reassuring smile.

"I can't go behind bars, mister," the farther one said nervously. He was pale with fright.

"Don't worry about it, boys. You can hack it—a lot of men have—and it sure as hell beats the alternative."

The frightened man shook his head, blinking rapidly.

"Just drop the guns, boys, and we can all relax," Longarm said calmly.

The man nearer him opened his fist and let his Winchester—it was a short saddle carbine, hardly an ideal choice for an ambusher with its short range and looping trajectory—fall into the mud.

"Now you," Longarm said softly.

The man's face twisted with terror, and his eyes grew wide.

*Ah, shit!* Longarm thought. He had seen it before. The man was more afraid of a cell's steel bars than of a lead slug in his gut. He was going to try it. And he had one man and two horses between himself and Longarm.

The man's hand, which had been on the cantle of his saddle, dropped out of sight, and he ducked.

Longarm fell to one knee and raised his Colt to aim below the bellies of the horses.

The sudden activity startled the animals, and they began to shuffle their feet and throw their heads.

For a long, long moment Longarm could not distinguish the pair of legs he wanted. Then the man scuttled sideways toward the rump of his horse. Longarm could see the butt of the man's rifle rise, and knew he had no time to waste.

The Colt roared, and a slug tore into the man's leg. He grunted and dropped to his side in the mud. The Winchester, Longarm noted, had fallen from his hand, and the fellow seemed to have no interest in it at the moment.

Longarm had very nearly forgotten the other man, and the inattention could have been fatal.

Only a few paces away, the other one was dragging at the grips of his pistol. He saw Longarm's eyes swing onto him. With a bellow of mingled fear and rage he hurtled himself forward across the few feet that separated them, his shoulder lowered and his hand still clawing at his gun.

The big Colt leaped in Longarm's fist for the second time, at point-blank range, and the heavy slug took the man square in the chest.

He began to fall, and Longarm had to step aside to avoid being struck by the already lifeless body as it splashed into the muck underfoot.

That one was dead, but the other had only been hit in the leg. He should still be able to provide some answers.

Longarm stepped to the side and looked carefully to make sure the man was not playing possum on him and did not have a pistol in his hand. The fallen Winchester still lay there in plain sight, but the man was curled on his side with his belly away from Longarm's view, and he could have

136

been holding half a dozen weapons concealed in front of him.

"You're covered and your partner's dead," Longarm said loudly. "I'd just as soon you didn't make me shoot you again."

The man did not move. He should have moaned or made some response. Longarm thought that he must indeed by lying doggo, still hoping for a chance to kill the deputy and get away.

The easy thing to do would be to put a finishing bullet into the fellow and take no chances. But the need was not clear. And he still wanted to be able to question him.

Longarm stepped softly to the other side of the wash bottom and inched his way forward, his Colt aimed and ready and his nerves on edge for the slightest sound or movement.

"Roll onto your back so I can see you better," Longarm ordered when he was in position above the man's head.

Again there was no response.

"Damn it, man, I'm gonna have to shoot you if you don't cooperate." He pulled the hammer of his Colt back, cocking it manually. It was not necessary with the weapon, but the sound was unmistakable in the stillness of the gully bottom.

Both threats were a bluff, but the wounded man would not know that.

Still there was no response.

"You're a stubborn son of a bitch, aren't you?" Longarm accused.

He allowed himself several unkind thoughts about the wounded ambusher but with a sigh resigned himself to cat-footing up onto the fellow. He wanted to take this one alive.

Longarm edged forward. He leaned over, trying to get a better view of the man's hands, but he could see nothing, neither empty hands nor weapons held against his belly there. Longarm took another step.

His angle of view was better now, and he could see the thick, red-brown mud the man had pooled below his waist.

*Damn,* Longarm thought bitterly.

137

He stepped forward and rolled the man onto his back. He was death-pale beneath a stubble of several days' beard growth, and his jeans were black with fresh, sticky blood.

Longarm's shot had taken him in the leg, but instead of merely disabling him, as Longarm had hoped, the bullet had severed a major artery. Some time during the fight, or perhaps while Longarm was creeping up on him and accusing him of playing possum, the man had died.

Longarm felt like spitting. It was bad enough that this pair had tried to kill him. It was worse that he could not question them about it.

And the day was just too damn hot for the labor that would be involved in loading these two onto their horses and taking them into town. By the time the ride was over, Longarm suspected, the bodies would have started to bloat and grow foul.

He was not looking forward to any of it, but postponing it would only make it worse. He rolled his sleeves up and remembered with a curse that his coat was still out there in the mud somewhere from when he had turned to tie it onto his gear and got distracted from that job instead. He would have to go looking for it before he could get these two on the road to their final resting place.

# Chapter 17

The deputy sheriff pulled his horse to a walk and then to a stop as they reached the edge of town. "Like I told you before, Deputy, we like to kill our own quail around here, so you just sit back and relax yourself. I'll pass along everything I find out. That's what the sheriff told me to do, and I follow my orders."

Longarm responded with a smile to the unfriendly glare the local deputy sent his way. He found himself wishing for the kind of cooperation he had gotten from the youngster Jaybird up in Elbert County.

Technically speaking, the assault on a Federal officer was a Federal crime and could have been pursued by Deputy Marshal Long with or without the consent of local authority.

But the policy was to avoid conflict unless there was a compelling reason to do otherwise. At this point, Longarm could not honestly claim an exemption from that rule, so he kept his mouth shut and his opinions silent.

They were entering Colorado City, the lower-class, slatternly sister of high-toned Colorado Springs just to the east.

Liquor was banned in the Springs, but it seemed to be a mainstay of the business community in Colorado City, judging at least from the number of saloon signs Longarm could see strung along the street before him.

The town serviced the mining trade farther up the mountains and was a center for transportation, both wagon and pack train, and mining equipment. It also provided entertainment, both the wet kind and the warm kind, for miners and teamsters down out of the hills.

It was set at the mouth of the principal pass leading into the Front Range between Denver and Pueblo, practically at the foot of Pikes Peak.

Longarm tilted his head back to look up to the top of the massive peak. Oddly enough, it was almost difficult from a point so near to be able to single out the feature that, from a greater distance, dominated the entire mountain range. Colorado City, though, was located at the base of the smaller, intervening mountains, practically unnoticed from a more distant perspective, but from here as eyecatching as the peak itself.

The pass and the toll road through it began at Colorado City although Manitou, slightly deeper into the mouth, was the actual jumping-off point for pack and wagon trains headed deep into the mountains for Fairplay and Leadville and the fabled high country gold camps.

It was nearly evening and Longarm could feel a breeze of cold air falling down through the pass to bring a chill through his salt-encrusted clothing. The contrast between this cool, fine evening breeze and the hot, almost humid morning's work was extreme. Longarm thought he could detect a faint, sharp, and most pleasant scent of snow-melt on the moving air here, and the slight odor made him wish for some of that high-country weather down here where the snows were long since melted and gone.

"Just don't go expecting too much," the deputy was saying. "Us local yokels aren't as damn well infallible as you Federal boys are supposed to be." He coughed into his fist. "O' course we don't go around arresting people just to get a case cleared, neither."

So that was what was prodding his pork, Longarm thought. Not an interest in superior law enforcement. Plain old jealousy was Longarm's guess. It was the deputy sheriff's problem and none of Custis Long's business.

"I told you before," the deputy rattled on, "I seen those fellows around, so I know they been here, but I can't put a name to neither of them, and their descriptions will fit half the men in Colorado City."

Longarm nodded. He knew he really should not, but he could not resist adding, "Even us Federal people can't expect miracles *every* time out."

The dig earned him a look of sheer loathing. "Come on, then."

If it made the guy shut up, Longarm decided, it was worth doing. He followed docilely behind and tied his horse at the hitch rail beside the deputy's.

"You can wait inside there," the reluctant assistant snapped. He pointed vaguely toward the storefronts beyond the railing.

"I'd rather . . ."

"I don't give a shit what you want, Deputy. I'll do my work by myself an' then I'll come and tell you what I've found out."

Longarm grunted. He could already guess how much information he was going to gain this way. But Billy Vail was not particularly fond of complaints about his people, and this laddybuck was just the kind who would delight in sending one off to Denver. Longarm did not want to give him the satisfaction. "It's your investigation, I reckon," he said.

"Damn right it is." The local stalked off down the board

sidewalk without another word.

"Thanks a whole bunch," Longarm muttered in his wake.

There were two lighted storefronts beyond the rail, and the deputy could have meant either one of them. One was a saloon and the other was an eatery. Longarm made a brief inspection of his stomach's rumblings and decided they were not bad enough to require immediate attention. He headed for the saloon.

"A bit of your very best Maryland rye, if you please," he told the bartender.

The fellow produced it without having to search around among the dusty, seldom-used bottles, and Longarm said, "Somebody around here has good taste."

"If you say so," the barkeep said.

Longarm savored the first warm taste of the whiskey and smiled. "It's all vile stuff, if you ask me," the bartender said.

"You don't drink?"

"Never." The man frowned and rubbed a wet towel across the hardwood surface of the bar.

"That's an odd admission for a man in your trade," Longarm observed. He reached into his pocket to pull out a cheroot. The bartender flicked a match and lighted it for him before Longarm could get out a match of his own. "Thanks." The fellow was mannerly enough, if a bit strange. "How come you're in the business, if you feel that way? If you don't mind my asking, that is."

The man grunted. "I don't mind." He fixed an eye on Longarm and asked, "You ever been up in those hills, ever done any prospecting?"

"As a matter of fact I have, a little."

"Then you oughta know. It's no fit way for a white man to make a living, I can tell you that. Even this's better. Steady pay. Regular hours. That counts for something."

Longarm nodded. He was not going to get into an argument about it, but the lure of boredom was something that had always escaped his understanding. And steady pay and regular hours seemed to be just another way to spell boredom. "Anyway," he said, "my opinion is that this is mighty fine fluid and welcome at the end of a hard day."

"Keeps me in business anyhow," the bartender grudgingly allowed. Another customer came to the other end of the bar and the man drifted away.

Longarm shook his head. Between the deputy sheriff and the bartender he was not at all sure what he thought about Colorado City. He took another drink of the excellent rye and decided not to worry about it.

More people were coming into the saloon now as the light faded from the sky and nearly all of the illumination available inside the place came from the pewter lamps hung on the walls and suspended from the ceiling. The doorway and window now were only blue-gray rectangles against the wall with no more light coming through them. The place began to get loud as it became busier, and soon a flock of soiled doves twittered in to laugh and giggle and squirm on the laps of the willing customers. Very few were going up the stairs for private parties this early in the evening, however. Longarm stood at the end of the bar with his back to a wall and observed the people at play.

A group of six men ejected a solitary drinker from a table, bought themselves three bottles of cheap whiskey, and settled down to a night of card playing.

At the other end of the room, becoming smokey by now, another group of freighters, or possibly miners—their boots said they were not horsebackers, whatever they did to get so dirty—began arguing over which among them would have the privilege of paying for the next round of drinks.

An argument like that was sure to attract the attention of the perfumed whores who were fluttering around the place, and within seconds there were four girls at the table of five men.

Longarm was amused. He did not have to be close to the men to know how ripe they smelled, yet the girls were eager enough to breathe that aroma as long as there was a dollar to be made from it. It seemed a high price to pay for a silver cartwheel.

Most of the whores were the usual dumpy, heavily pow-
dered, suety-bodied type who frequent such places, but one
of them must have been new to the trade. In the poor light
given by the badly trimmed lamps, she looked almost pretty.

Several of the freighters seemed to think so too because
three of them began pulling at her, wanting her to sit in
their laps and wiggle them into a state of excitement.

The girl seemed to be frightened rather than pleased,
although Longarm would have expected her to line them up
one at a time—or take them upstairs all at once if she was
feeling wicked enough for that—and make sure she got
some money from each of the interested parties.

Instead, though, she began to pull away from the grasping
hands, and her young face took on a haunted look that was
not pleasant to see. Longarm set his glass down.

Two of the men were on their feet now, each with a firm
grasp on the girl's arm. The third man stood and began
arguing with the other two. Longarm was too far away and
there was too much noise in the place for him to hear what
was being said, but the expressions were enough to tell him
what was going on.

The third man grabbed for the girl. She tried to twist
away, but with the other two holding her she could not go
very far. She managed only to jerk herself back so that the
man's hand closed on the bodice of her red dress.

Her breasts were small and sagged low against her scrawny
chest. She was pale and had the poor, loose muscle tone
that comes from inactivity and cheap food. She looked very
small and very vulnerable with her dress torn and pulled
down to her waist.

"Please! Please don't, mistuh!" She was yelling it loud
enough to be heard through the noise of the saloon.

The scrap had caught the attention of the other drinkers
in the place now, and they were beginning to laugh and
shout encouragement, most of it directed toward the freighters, asking them to remove more of the girl's dress.

She looked very young and, incredibly, she began to
blush. Longarm would not have thought it possible for a

whore to blush, but this one was managing it.

One of the freighters slapped her, a long backhanded blow, and a stream of blood showed at the corner of her painted mouth. The man repeated it with a hard slash across her small breasts, and Longarm could see the girl's face go white with pain.

Hell, he told himself with disgust. It's a bitch when a man finds himself in a fuss over a common whore. But even a hog has feelings. He took another sip of the good rye and drifted across the room toward the noisy group.

The physical one of the freighters—he was a big son of a bitch and had the muscle you like to see in a good ox— was raring back to take another swing at the terrified girl.

Longarm reached forward and touched him lightly on the arm.

"Not a good idea, neighbor," he said mildly. "I think the young lady's kinda bitten off more than she wants to chew here, so why don't you let her go get herself covered. Then she can come back and work your table a little calmer, if she wants." He was smiling and speaking softly.

"What business is it of yours?" the big man demanded belligerently.

Longarm sighed. He reached into his coat and brought out his wallet, but he flipped it open only briefly. There damn sure was no Federal crime being committed here, and he did not think it necessary to let the gentlemen get too long a look at his badge. "Just keeping a little order here, boys. There's no need for any excitement."

He motioned to the men. "If you boys would just kinda turn loose of her there. That's fine, thanks. And you, young lady, I suggest you run along and get something to cover yourself before you get back to your duties." He smiled. "There's such a thing as too much of a good thing, you see. Causes riots and all sorts of nonsense, and I don't expect we want any of that tonight, do we?" He slipped an arm around the girl's waist, pointed her toward the stairs, and gave her a gentle push.

She got the message quickly enough and bolted from the

group and up the stairs like a mountain sheep running up a cliff face.

"See there, boys? No fuss, no trouble. Have a pleasant evening, now."

Longarm started to turn away, but the big man grabbed him by the coatsleeve and yanked him back around to face them.

Longarm looked pointedly down at the powerful fist clenched in the fabric of his coat and then back up into its owner's grimy face. "You do like to live dangerous, don't you boy?" He was smiling again, but now there was a glint of gunmetal steel in the blue of his eyes.

"What I like to do," the big man said, "is to beat the shit oughta wiseass lawmen like you."

Longarm grinned and shook his head. "And go through all that pain? I'm surprised at you."

The man laughed. "You gotta still be on your feet to arrest me, lawboy."

The grin spread. "Oh, I doubt we'll have to go through all those formalities. I expect we can settle it between us."

"Did you hear that, boys? The lawboy here says he can whip Blacksnake Hoolihan. Now, ain't that the funniest thing you ever heard? Shit!" He shoved his face within an inch of Longarm's nose and made a growling sound.

"Is that supposed to scare me away?"

"Only if you got the brains of a cur dog, lawboy. Which I don't think you do. So put 'em up and I'll thrash the shit plumb out of you."

"It's a fact, Blacksnake, that most of the curs I've seen lately have been just as feisty as hell. But it's also a fact that I have no intention of splitting my knuckles on your ugly face. So I think we'll end this without a lot of kicking and biting and fisticuffs, all right?"

The big man found himself looking into the .44.

"You see, Blacksnake," Longarm went on in that same mild voice, "I don't really fight fair. I fight to win, or not at all."

146

The big man was cussing and snarling, but he was also backing quickly away.

"Like I said, boys, have yourselves a pleasant evening." Longarm nodded toward them politely—they were a much more subdued group now—and turned to go, but again he was stopped by a hand on his arm.

This time, though, the hand was small and lightly applied. It belonged to one of the whores.

"There's somebody upstairs who would like to see you, mister."

# Chapter 18

Longarm was more than half expecting to be led to the skinny little whore in one of the "working" rooms upstairs, but the bawd took him past those to another flight of stairs behind a door that looked like it led to just another bedroom.

At the top of the stairs he stepped into a suite of living quarters that was as elegantly appointed as anything he had seen in the Antlers Hotel over in posh Colorado Springs. He did not stop and stare, though, until he saw the room's occupant.

Expecting a scrawny slattern, he was greeted instead by a tall, stately woman in evening dress who easily overcame her quarters for sheer elegance. She was wearing jewelry that would knock a mule's eyes out from the dazzle and glitter. He hoped it was paste, because nobody should risk that kind of money in plain sight if the gems were real.

The woman herself was full-bodied, her cleavage a snowy valley between mountain peaks. Her hair was raven and was piled in a confusingly intricate mass on top of a heart-stopping face. Longarm came to a dead halt and found himself staring. He recovered enough to snatch his hat off.

"Ma'am?"

She retained her seat and motioned him with a graceful turn of her wrist to a chair facing hers across a low table. Her manner managed to turn an ordinary wingback chair with brocade upholstery into something approaching a throne in its effect.

"I am Melinda Coogan. *Mrs*. Coogan. Thank you for joining me." Her voice was low and throaty and held out hints of smoky promise.

Longarm introduced himself.

Mrs. Coogan laughed. "I knew it could not be any of our local officers when they told me a badge was produced. None of them would have lifted a finger to help that poor child."

Longarm glanced around the room. The "poor child" was not in evidence here, and the girl who had escorted him had gone. "It was no bother," he said.

"Of course it was a bother, Marshal, or it would not have aroused my curiosity. Would you mind standing?"

"What?"

"I asked..."

"Oh, I heard you, all right." He shrugged and did as she requested.

Melinda Coogan tented her fingertips beneath her chin and peered at him from head to foot and slowly back again. "Broad shoulders," she said. "Narrow hips. Good length of leg. You are a very attractive man, Marshal. No doubt any one of my girls would be delighted to spend the night with you."

"Should I thank you for all that?" Longarm was beginning to know how a steer must feel when it is put onto the auction

149

block. Or a whore in the doorway of her crib.

The woman smiled. "You don't like that, do you, Marshal?"

"No."

"But I think you are sensitive enough to see my point in the observations. That, you see, makes it all the more interesting to me that you would have gone to the trouble you did for one of my girls." She shrugged. "I was curious, as I said. I dislike questions without answers, and so I asked you up here."

"You are the owner of this place, then?"

"This one and another in Colorado City. Half a dozen cribs in Fairplay. Ten cribs and a small house in Leadville. A girl alone has to make her way in the world, you know."

Longarm smiled. "So I've heard. But you said it was Mrs. Coogan. Widowed?"

She looked uninterested in the question. "Who knows. Possibly by now I am. You may have heard of my husband, or former husband, Jack."

"I think I have."

"I should expect so. Bless his penny-ante dark soul, the poor thing is wanted in most of the states and all the territories of the Union for one thing or another, none of them amounting to anything of consequence."

"Jack isn't in residence here, though?"

Melinda laughed again, louder and quite heartily. "Marshal, I believe you were prepared to make an arrest."

He smiled. "I still am if I see him."

"I *like* you, Marshal Long. But you can relax. I haven't seen Jack for several years. The last time he tried to put the touch on me, I had him thrown out. I doubt that he will ever be back."

Longarm nodded. "So tell me, Mrs. Coogan, has your curiosity been satisfied? I had a bottle downstairs . . ."

". . . of Maryland rye," she finished for him. She gestured toward a sideboard. "Would you mind pouring for both of us? The champagne for me, please."

Longarm was not sure whether he was intrigued by this

150

beautiful woman or repulsed by her. But he went to the sideboard. There was a fresh bottle of his favorite rye there, and a green-colored bottle of champagne chilling in a bucket of shaved ice. Mrs. Coogan knew how to live well, that was for certain.

He wrestled the cork out of the champagne bottle without making a fool of himself or spewing it all over the Oriental carpet and poured himself a large measure of the rye. "There you are. Would you mind if I smoked?"

"Not at all."

He lit up and sat back in the chair, conscious now of his mud-spattered appearance after the morning's fight. He had not yet had a chance to clean up.

"Have you eaten, Marshal Long?"

"No, I haven't, but—"

"Please. I would enjoy your company, although I eat only a light supper. I would like you to share it with me."

He shrugged. What the hell? He had nothing better to do.

Melinda rang a silver bell, and a moment later a rather large colored girl in a gray uniform and crisply starched apron appeared in one of the doorways leading out of the sitting room. "Supper for two, Carrie."

The service took little more than a minute. There were fruits and cheeses and cold meats. Melinda picked at the food with little interest, giving most of her attention to Longarm while he ate. The meal was about as satisfying as the free lunch downstairs would have been.

"I've been thinking about this, Marshal. I believe I owe you a debt of gratitude for your help. Please select any one of my girls for the entire night. There will be no charge, of course."

He shook his head.

"If you prefer young boys, I could arrange that too."

Longarm laughed. "You don't have to work so hard at being wicked. You aren't going to shock me. You won't entice me, either, though."

She raised her eyebrows.

151

"Let me put this a polite way. I don't use a comb tied to the string by a bunkhouse mirror either, nor another man's toothbrush."

"I see. You claim to be fastidious, then, instead of virtuous. That's good. I don't trust virtue."

"What do you trust?" he asked, curious.

"Cash."

"I'm afraid I can't be of much interest to you, then. A Federal employee sees little enough of that."

"On the contrary, Marshal Long, you interest me very much." She shook her head and for a moment an expression of raw bitterness flickered across those handsome features.

"What were you going to say?"

"Nothing."

"I don't believe you."

"Then believe that is none of your affair, Marshal. That you can believe."

"All right." He took another drink of the excellent rye. "Would you like a refill?"

"Please."

They sat in silence for several minutes, and Longarm found that he was wondering what this odd woman was thinking about. She kept looking at him with an expression he could not begin to read.

"Would you...?" she began, but she cut herself short.

"Go ahead."

She looked away for a moment. When she looked back at him, she was composed and seemed sure of herself again. "Your clothing, Marshal. You look almost disreputable."

"It was a long day."

"It is much too late to have them cleaned anywhere in town. I could have it done for you."

"That would present the problem of what I should wear, and where I should wear it, in the meantime."

"I have a suggestion." She was no longer at all sure of herself, he saw. If anything she looked...He had to search for it, and when he finally realized what it was, it seemed very much out of place in this woman. She seemed *shy*.

152

"Or do you have the same objection to me as you would have to one of my girls?"

"I can imagine you doing a lot of things, Melinda, but I don't think that is among them."

"You are perceptive, Marshal. Very nearly accurate, anyway. There was a time, years ago, when Jack used me in some of his scams. You know: set the mark up when his wife is out of town. Then my vengeful husband would burst in at the last moment. I will admit to you, Jack's timing was not always what it should have been. He seemed to find that amusing, and I finally began to suspect that in his perverse way he was being honest with the mark and giving him something for his money. We quit that scam soon afterward."

"There are some fellows," Longarm said without thinking, "who like . . ." He shut up.

"Taking a woman recently used by another man? It's not uncommon. *Nothing* is as uncommon as the sick ones believe it is. All of their quirks are shared by many others, no matter how outlandish." She did not sound especially sympathetic toward them.

"And your quirks, Melinda?"

"I have none."

"I find that hard to believe," he said.

"It is as true as it is unfortunate. But I still do have a desire sometimes to touch and to fondle and to speak French, if you know what I mean, with a handsome and gallant gentleman. Which is why I would like you to stay, if you would want to after you understand my situation."

"Now I don't understand. I thought I did until just now, but . . ."

Again the bitterness was etched across her face. "Did you wonder why I did not rise to greet you, Marshal? Or why I asked a guest to pour my wine? I could have called for Carrie. Or I could have asked you to do it for me."

She slammed a fist down on her knee. It should have hurt, but she did not flinch.

"Four years ago, Marshal, during one of Jack's famous

153

getaways, our buggy overturned at high speed. A wheel struck me in the back." She touched herself a few inches below her breasts. "From this point on downward, Marshal, you could grind your cigar out against my flesh and I would never know it until the smell reached me. I have no feeling at all."

"None?"

"Believe me, I have tried everything. If you choose to stay, you shall have to carry me to bed, Marshal."

He remembered the large serving girl. Her presence, and her size, made sense now.

"Of course, none of that makes me incapable of giving pleasure, Marshal. And, as I said, I do enjoy the privilege of touching now and then. Very rarely, I'm afraid. There are not many men who want to waste their time screwing half a woman."

"Somehow, Melinda, I really don't think you're anything less than a complete woman." He stood and bent to pick her up in his arms. "Which way are we going?"

Hours later, his clothes already cleaned and pressed and hanging on the door of her ornate wardrobe, he raised his lips from her nipple and dragged the hairs of his mustache down her throat and across the sensitive surfaces of her breasts. Twice already she had shudderingly claimed to have reached satisfaction from his manipulations of her breasts, and he wondered if they had become more sensitive through the years, the way a blind man's hearing seems to become more acute after he loses his vision.

"You're a good man, Custis Long. It's a shame you insist on a straight way of life." She chuckled. "If you would ever consider becoming a kept man . . ."

"I appreciate the invitation, but I guess I'll pass."

"Damn. You do believe in virtue, after all, don't you?"

"Guilty," he confessed.

"Is your job that important to you?"

"Yes." That was it, as simple as that. No elaboration was necessary.

She sighed and snuggled closer to him. "What are you working on now, Deputy Marshal?"

He told her.

"And that fool Lonnie is supposed to be out getting information for you? I hope you aren't counting on much."

"Frankly, I'm not."

"Tell me about those men again." She hesitated. "There isn't much that goes on in the City that I don't know about sooner or later."

He told her, and she reached out for the silver bell that was always at her side. Carrie came in, and Melinda gave her a terse string of orders. "Quickly now."

A pleasant hour later the answers were back.

"The men were called Blue Pete and Roper. If they had other names, they were never used around here. They weren't much account. Two nights ago they were seen at the High Hat talking with a pair of cowboys who weren't dressed much better than they were. They left town that same night and haven't been seen since."

"Are they sure about that, Carrie?"

The colored girl shrugged. "Who can be sure? That's what the word is."

Melinda waited until the girl had gone, then nuzzled Longarm's neck. She began to move lower and lower, her tongue darting out and back into the warm softness of her mobile mouth. She reached the object of her attentions and touched him reverently. "You can pay me now," she said.

Longarm did not mind. It didn't even have to go on the expense sheet.

# Chapter 19

Longarm had learned to hate assumptions. There is nothing like a man's own assumption to send him away from the facts onto a wild-goose chase into the realms of fancy. And that, by damn, was what he had been doing right along here. Making assumptions. Assuming something was so just because everyone believed it was so, or because it *seemed* to be so. Or because something *seemed* to be logical and ordinary.

Assumptions were so disgustingly often wrong. While simple, basic, ordinary common sense so often was not. Particularly when that common sense was in conflict with the damnable *assumptions* of a case.

Deputy United States Marshal Custis Long felt much

better when he rode out of Colorado City the next morning. It was, he thought, one of the finest mornings he could remember in some time. Both in what he was riding away from—a handsome and very talented woman named Melinda—and in what he was riding toward—an end to this case at long last.

A broad smile showed starkly white against the windburnt brown of his face and mustache when he finally reached his destination and knocked on the door.

"Yes, Marshal?"

He took his hat off. "G'day, Mrs. Crowder. Might I come in?"

"Of course." She stepped back. "Could I fix you some lunch?"

"No thanks. I came to have a word with you."

"From the amount of time you've spent here, I daresay you must think I am a primary suspect in your investigation."

"Not a suspect, ma'am, but I'd say you might be a key to it."

"Really? I am anxious to hear this."

"Well, ma'am, the way you could help would be to help me capture that buckskin horse."

Catherine Crowder looked disgusted. "A few nights ago, Marshal Long, you made a promise to me. Already you are breaking it. I told you then and I tell you now, I shall *not*—"

"No, ma'am, you misunderstood me. What I promised you was that I wouldn't ask for your help so I could *kill* that horse. And what I just now asked you was would you give me a hand to capture him. There's a world of difference there."

"But I thought—"

"Yes, ma'am. So does everyone else. But I'm not exactly a government game hunter. I was sent down here to catch a murderer, not a wild horse. Killing the rogue was a sort of side issue. As it happens, I need that son of a gun as a witness."

157

"A *witness?*"

Longarm grinned. "Yes, ma'am. Old Buck is going to be a star witness for the prosecution in this here case. Assuming I can find him and get him here alive. And that's where you come in.

"In all the claptrap I've heard about that horse, the only real solid information based on eyewitness account is the facts that, one, he sure enough did kill Lew Chance up near the Denver stockyards and, two, after that he showed up here and you hand-fed this terror of the plains. Which means that he may or may not put up with strangers and menfolk but it is a proven fact that he gets along with you. You follow me?"

She nodded.

"So what I had in mind was for me to hire you as a sort of guide—on the government payroll, of course—to catch that critter and bring him here to do his witnessing."

"And you wouldn't shoot him?"

"No, ma'am, I sure wouldn't. That's a promise too, and I'm not much for breaking my given word."

"I don't know if you could manage it even with my help, Marshal. After all, practically every cowman around here has tried to find where Bucky takes those cattle he steals. They have followed his trail as far as possible and ridden for miles and miles beyond hoping to find him and kill him. I don't see how . . ."

Longarm was grinning again. "I don't think it's going to be all that difficult, ma'am."

"But—"

"You see, ma'am, all those trails've been leading off east onto the plains. Everybody knows you can't track out there worth a darn this time of year, and everybody knows you could ride within half a mile of a thousand-head herd and not see it for the way the land rolls. So nobody's been surprised that they haven't found the stallion or those stolen cows."

"That's true enough."

"Sure it is," Longarm said. "And, like a blind man, I've

been following right along with the rest of the crowd on that same assumption. Assuming that the horse and the cattle were heading off out into that dry, dusty, hot, windy country east of here.

"Well, a cool breeze the other night an' a belated realization that assumptions are dangerous things finally put me to thinking about not where that particular buckskin horse was going with his stolen cattle, but where *any* wild animal with a grain of common horse sense would go if he was free of man's control."

"And you think you know where he is just because of that?" she asked.

"Yes, ma'am. It remains to be proven, of course, but I surely do think that I can find that horse now. Will you help me?"

She smiled. "Marshal Long, I believe that I will." She held her hand out to shake on the bargain.

# Chapter 20

They stopped to water the horses in an icy fall of water that still carried the scent of snow. The trail here followed the path of the stream, and the sound of the racing water was a pleasant undertone for every step of the way.

"Could we take a break here ourselves?" Catherine Crowder asked.

"Of course." Longarm dismounted and helped the woman down from her sidesaddle.

They stood with slack reins while Mrs. Crowder's stocky bay drank briefly. Longarm's horse smelled the water but was not interested in it.

"It's beautiful up here, isn't it?" Catherine said. She looked around toward the peaks that surrounded them. Here, deep into the mountains, the peaks were not impressive individually, but in a mass they marched away into the distance in stately order. She raised her face to the sky and breathed in. "Even the air feels good—clean and cool and refreshing." She smiled. "In another few years my place down on the plains will be proven and title issued. I think I might sell it then and take up some land here."

"A person could do worse. The winters aren't as bad as they're made out to be, either."

"I shall certainly give it some thought." She let her reins fall and walked with a light, springy step to a fallen log nearby. Longarm was reminded again—as if he needed yet another reminder after two full days in her company—of what an attractive woman she was. The hint of gray in her auburn hair seemed to add to her beauty, and there was that undeniable aura of sensuality about her. Still, she had given no indication that she thought of him as a man—only as an officer with a job to do.

He sat on the log a few feet away from her, pulled out a cheroot, and lighted it.

"Doesn't it get boring?" she asked.

"Beg pardon?"

"Doesn't it get boring? All the stopping and questioning and never learning anything, I mean. We have stopped at every cabin and dugout between here and Manitou. I would think it would become boring after a while."

Longarm shrugged. "Finding an answer to a question is hardly exciting, but it's a big part of the job. A lawman has to use his patience much more often than his guns, that's for sure. But patience and a refusal to quit: that's the main edge we have over the bad guys, ma'am. They want things easy. We want things done. We have to be willing to work at it or they'll have it all over us, every time."

She smiled. "You certainly don't do much to promote your job as a glamorous one, Marshal."

"It isn't glamorous, ma'am, but it sure is necessary. I'm not ashamed of what I do nor how I do it. I don't feel any need to lie about it."

She thought about that for a moment. "I like your attitude, Marshal." She made a face. "Really, I am becoming tired of addressing you by your title all the time. What do people usually call you? If you don't mind my asking."

"I don't mind at all, ma'am. Mostly they call me Longarm, for fairly obvious reasons."

She laughed. "Yes, with the kind of patience I have seen lately, I can well understand how they would. Are you really good at your job?"

"I do my best, ma'am. So far it's been good enough that they keep on paying me."

"I suspect you are very good indeed. Would you do me a favor, Longarm?"

"Ask it first. Then I can tell you."

"If I am going to call you Longarm, would you please call me Catherine? 'Ma'am' makes me feel old. I don't care for that, even if I *am* older than you."

He looked away from her. "Old, ma'am—excuse me, Catherine—is not something I would consider you to be. Far from it."

"Was that a compliment, Longarm?"

"Uh-huh."

"In that case, I thank you."

There was a silence between them that became awkward as it lengthened. Longarm was uncomfortably aware of the direction his own thoughts were taking, but he had no clue as to what hers might be. He doubted seriously that they were anything remotely like his carnal speculations.

She was the one who broke the silence, finally. "Should we go now?" She stood up.

"Yes, ma'am."

She did not correct him.

Longarm helped her back into her saddle and swung onto his horse. They headed west along the rutted wagon trail again.

Three-quarters of an hour later he was grinning broadly as he came out of a small trading post and rejoined her. "Good news," he said.

"You found him?"

"I don't know; you'll have to tell me that for sure when we get a look at him. But the old boy who runs this place said he heard some Utes talking about a good-looking buckskin they wanted to get their hands on. And down south of here there's a rancher who has been complaining that there's a wild stud in the neighborhood trying to run off his best mares."

"Do you think it's Bucky, then?"

Longarm shrugged. "Sure seems possible." He looked around. "I tell you what, though. If I was a stallion running wild, I'd sure rather be up here where the grass is good and the water is cool than down in that dry, brown country below. You just bet I would."

"And for your mares, Longarm?"

Longarm could not have sworn that he blushed—in fact, he would have vehemently denied that he was capable of it—but he would have had to admit to feeling a certain amount of warmth in his cheeks at that unexpected question.

"Why, ma'am," he answered truthfully enough, "I reckon I would just have to try to steal some." He turned away and gave his attention to his horse.

They rode south from the store, and a few miles further on they came to the biggest tree stump Longarm had seen in many a year. The stump was a strangely colored yellow-white that looked out of place and almost unnatural.

"The wood from that must've made a lot of fires," he said.

"If there was such a thing as fire then," Catherine said.

"What?"

She smiled and reined her bay toward the huge stump. "Take a closer look, Longarm."

He did, going so far as to dismount and touch it in his disbelief. "Why, that's not a stump at all. That's solid rock!"

Catherine shook her head. "Not really. The wood is petrified. It's wood, all right, but so old that it's turned to stone. Or so I understand. There is some question about the process. What is undeniable is that that stump is older than

163

mankind. The wood from that tree built no houses, and if there was fire to consume it that long ago it was caused by lightning. No human ever felt its heat."

"I'll be damned. Oh—sorry, ma'am."

"Have you given up on calling me Catherine?"

He grinned. "I'll try to remember."

"It would be ungallant of you to refuse my request now."

Longarm remounted and they continued south, the slope of the land trending downward here among the low peaks. They picked up another stream to follow and passed several huge formations of dark gray granite before they entered a grassy depression of the kind the old-timers called parks.

"What a lovely spot," Catherine said.

"You won't get me to argue," Longarm said. He looked off to the right. The sun had already disappeared behind a high, forested ridgeline. "I expect we should think about making camp somewhere, unless you want to keep on going until we find a ranch or cabin or something civilized."

"Considering how long it has been since we saw the last house, that might take all night or even longer. I think we would be better off to make camp."

"Over there looks good enough. There's wood and water, and if the wind comes up that hill will give us shelter."

"Whatever you say, Longarm. I'm no expert in this."

He took the lead then, unsaddled and hobbled the horses, and got a fire started to begin making coals while he gathered enough wood to burn well into the night and have enough left over for a breakfast fire as well.

"You're very efficient, aren't you?" Catherine said, watching his sure, economical movements as he worked.

"I never thought about it, exactly. You might be able to make a case for me being lazy, though. I like to get things done as quick and easy as possible. Don't care much for having to redo something already done once."

"That is what I said."

"Okay." He brought water in the coffee pot, and Catherine took over the duties of cooking. By the time their meal was done it was fully dark. The dome of the night sky overhead was a deep velvet black studded generously with the bright pinpricks of stars. The sky seemed very close here.

They ate slowly and in silence, but this time the silence was a comfortable and companionable one. When they finished and the tin plates were washed clean Longarm lighted a cheroot from the fire and stood.

"I'll take a little walk now, Catherine, if you'd like to get ready to turn in."

"I won't be but a minute," she said.

He walked to the top of the hill under which they had camped. He was as fit as a man was likely to be, but even so he could feel the pull of the elevation in his lungs, and he slowed as he neared the top.

A slight breeze was blowing. The moving air was cold against his skin, despite the season. It felt fresh and good to him after the dry heat of the plains.

Somewhere off to the north he could hear two coyotes dueling with their short, choppy yaps, and somewhere nearer he could hear the crash of a heavy body moving through brush, possibly an elk that had caught his scent and been alarmed. There was no moon, only the starlight to see by, and in all the vast amount of land that stretched out before him he could see neither lamp nor firelight except what he had made himself. He took a pull on the cheroot and drew the smoke into his lungs. He felt a deep contentment that had nothing to do with the cigar. After several minutes he turned and walked back down the hill to the warmth of the fire.

Catherine was tucked into her bedroll with her saddle for a pillow. Her soogan—it would have belonged to her husband, Longarm guessed—was tucked in chin-high. The firelight caught her eyes, and he knew she was awake and watching him.

"Comfortable?" he asked.

"Reasonably so." She hesitated. "Could I ask you something, Longarm?"

"Of course."

165

"Does . . . does my age repulse you?"

"I don't hardly believe you asked me that. Of course it don't."

"You don't find me unattractive?"

"Anything but. You're a fine-looking woman, Catherine Crowder. I don't find it easy keeping my place around you. I'm sorry, but you asked, and that's the truth of it. Not that you need to be afraid of me. I don't mean that either. It's just . . ."

"I know what you mean." She smiled. "The truth is, I'm glad. Would you think it terribly forward of me, Longarm, if I told you that my husband has been gone for some time now? And that I am not carved from ice? I think you are a good and a decent man, Custis Long. And a most attractive one."

He turned to her. "I wouldn't think badly of you at all," he said.

Catherine Crowder nodded. She looked solemn and a bit shy. A hand crept out from under the folds of her soogan, and she pulled it aside.

She was nude beneath the covers. She stood slowly, her trim body coiling and rising gracefully, and she posed in the firelight like a perfectly wrought statue, her long limbs cleanly formed and her breasts, firm and sharp-tipped, in perfect proportion to her small waist and the swell of her hips.

Her belly, very slightly convex, was satin-textured. It fell away to a softly curling vee of pubic hair that had a roan appearance from the mingling of auburn and gray. Droplets of eager moisture dampened the salt-and-pepper hair, and Longarm found himself being stirred by the sight of her. His erection was immediate.

"You're beautiful," he whispered. He meant it.

She smiled and held her arms out to him, waiting where she was for him to come and claim her.

He moved to her and ran his fingertips over her body. Catherine closed her eyes and tipped her head back. Her throat, corded from the intensity of what she must have been

166

feeling, was exposed and vulnerable. He bent his lips to that vulnerability and lightly nibbled at the taut column of flesh.

He stroked and petted her, and her teeth bit into the fullness of her underlip. Finally he embraced her and covered her mouth with his.

The taste of her was as sweet as he had imagined it would be, and he lowered her gently back onto the waiting blankets.

Catherine's hands crept between them, cupping and stroking his scrotum, tracing the length of him, nipping playfully at the tiny slit at the tip of his member.

"I hope you are in no hurry," she whispered.

"No. None at all."

They touched and tasted endlessly, in a void of time, while the stars circled silently and unheeded overhead. Each touch was a pleasure and each newly discovered pleasure was good for its own sake, each exploration leading ultimately toward a climax that would have to come at some distant time in the future, but Longarm found himself wanting to delay that time as long as would be humanly possible, because with this woman the journey was far more important than the destination.

They could have lain like that for minutes or for hours— he had no way of knowing and cared even less—before, without consciously willing it, he found himself sliding slowly into the warm depths of her. It was not so much that Longarm entered her as that Catherine absorbed him into her own flesh.

He pressed deep into her and lay with his body entirely on top of hers, both of them with their legs pressed together, his flesh joined with hers. They lay without moving.

Catherine moved her head away from his neck, where he had been enjoying the feel of her breath on his skin. She smiled at him. "Be very still now, if you can."

Longarm nodded.

Slowly, very slowly, Catherine began to move her hips. Longarm tried to remain immobile, although it took all of

167

his will power to accomplish that feat.

The heat of her body was intense, the chill of the night air so deep into the mountains a startling contrast. Each time she pulled away from him the cold air reached him, and each time she pressed her belly against his to draw him back into her depths the heat was searing. The contrasting sensations built him higher and higher, but the repeated chill seemed to prevent him from reaching the brink and spilling into her. He clenched his teeth and gripped her shoulders in a powerful clasp, unmindful of the bruises he must be leaving there.

He felt her breath and her body quicken. "Now," she whispered fiercely.

The slow, measured control was abandoned, and Catherine began to buck and pump wildly beneath him.

Longarm's self-control was gone as well, and he joined her in a frenzy of lunging plunges.

He reached the summit of his endurance and spewed a flood of hot fluid that seemed to pulse and flow uninterrupted for half of an eternity.

He was dimly aware of Catherine's climax as her body convulsed beneath him and she bit hard into the pad of muscle on the top of his right shoulder. She was still moaning and whimpering when, spent, he collapsed onto her.

It was hours longer before they slept.

# Chapter 21

They got a slow start the next morning, and rode south along the stream for several hours before turning back.

"Why aren't we going on that way?" Catherine asked.

Longarm grinned at her. "We haven't just been riding, you know. We've been looking for tracks. Haven't seen any."

"Really? Personally, I have been looking for a horse."

"The chances of riding up to him are pretty slim. We're more likely to see his tracks first, then find where he uses during the day. This country ahead of us now is pretty rugged."

She nodded. "I certainly can't argue with that." For half an hour their horses had been making poor time picking their way over and around gray rock formations and scrambling down rocky chutes that would lead ultimately to the Arkansas River miles to the south.

"We're trying to use horse sense, remember? Why would a wild, free animal choose to be down here when there is all that good grass in the parks up where we camped?"

She shrugged.

"Right. No reason at all. So we go back."

"But . . ."

"Why this particular route? We've been following the creek. He has to come to water. Well, we know he hasn't been coming to this particular creek, or we'd have seen some sign. So now we go back to that little feeder creek. Remember it? It joins this one not far from where we camped. We'll follow that one for a while and see if we do any better."

"It makes sense when you explain it."

"Common sense," he agreed. "I get mad at myself every time I forget to use it and get carried away with assumptions."

They had lunch at the campsite they had used the night before and headed out again. Catherine dropped a few delicately worded hints that she would have been willing to take an after-lunch nap, two to a bedroll, but Longarm pretended not to understand and pulled the cinches tight on the horses. There was a job to be done. There would be time enough for play afterward.

The smaller thread of clear water ran down from the west by northwest, spread here and there by a beaver dam that spilled the cold water across islands of bright green in the otherwise pale green of the high mountain grasses. A man who took up land here would be able to cut hay for his winter feed, Longarm saw. The beaver, once almost gone from these mountains, was coming back, and the land was responding. It had probably been forty years since the fur brigades trapped this area and wintered in its parks.

*If you was a horse,* Longarm told himself, *or just the*

*kind of man who could be content to settle in to one place
and one woman for the rest of your time . . .* He refused to
finish the thought.

"Hold up a minute," he said sharply.

"What is it?" She sounded frightened and he paused to
reassure her.

"Nothing to worry about. I just don't want these horses
walking on the tracks over there."

Catherine smiled. "You are a very intense man when you
are working, Marshal Long."

"Back to that name, are we, ma'am?"

She laughed. "I'll show you later."

"Is that a promise?"

Catherine stopped her horse, and Longarm edged his
forward so he could get a better look at the depressions left
in the soft ground beside the beaver pond they were skirting.

So far they had found—he had found, really—countless
deer and elk tracks and more than a few footprints left by
bear. There had even been a few marks left by large cats.

These, though, were unmistakably the tracks of horses
coming to water. And from what the storekeeper had told
him, and his own observations of the inky blackness around
them the night before, it seemed unlikely that any rancher's
horse herd would have been this far south of the wagon trail
through Ute and Wilkerson Passes.

"This could be the old gentleman right here," Longarm
said, with more than a tinge of pleasure in his voice.

"Are you sure?" Catherine bumped her horse up beside
him and sat staring down at the deep imprints.

Longarm shook his head. "No, but I reckon we'll know
soon enough. It looks like he came out of that draw over
there. If it was him, that is. I'm counting on you to tell me
that."

They turned south again and rode between two low hills.
The gravel soil underfoot had been disturbed, but it was
impossible to tell for sure what kind of animal had left the
disturbance. The loose gravel would not take a firm print.

Still, Longarm was fairly sure this would have to be the path taken by the horse that had come to the creek behind them.

He began to wonder if he should have left his McClellan saddle behind and hired a heavier stock saddle with a horn for roping. If the buckskin put up a fight to avoid capture...if it was the buckskin they were tracking...He shrugged. It was too late to think about that now. But sometimes habit could be as bad as assumption in this line of work.

A grassy bottom meandered between the rocky, forested hills here, and they followed the grass, Longarm's eyes sweeping into the fringes of cool shade along their path. It was midafternoon and a smart, free horse might want to enjoy the cool comfort of the shade at this time of day.

A quarter of a mile ahead, Longarm's careful search found a flicker of motion. It could have been nothing more than the flutter of a magpie's wings, but he looked again more closely.

He grinned. "Down there," he said. "Can you see them?"

"Where?"

He pulled his horse close against hers and pointed. Catherine sighted down his arm and pointing finger. "I think—Yes, I do see them. Two horses."

"Four," he corrected. "There's the two you're looking at. They're right at the edge of the trees. Look to the left and a little deeper into the trees, behind that blowdown. There's another, and then left again about twenty yards there's a fourth."

She shook her head. "I really can't see but the two. Is any of them Bucky, do you think?"

"No, they're all sorrels or browns, maybe a bay over there to the left. None of them's a buckskin, for sure."

"What do we do now?"

"We just keep riding. They've seen us and they haven't spooked, so we know they're familiar with horseback riders and aren't afraid. So we just keep going at this same pace. We don't want them to think we're chasing them."

172

Catherine's bay raised its muzzle and whickered as it caught the scent of the strange horses. A moment later there was an answering squeal from somewhere back in the trees. Longarm pulled to a halt and motioned for Catherine to do the same. That was a stud horse's challenge, and Longarm was damned glad neither of them was mounted on another stallion, or there would be a fight coming.

He could see movement deep in the shaded stand of wood, and a tawny shape trotted out into the open with a high, prancing step.

It was a buckskin stud, all right, though much heavier-bodied and prouder of appearance than the horse in the picture Longarm carried.

This one had a long mane, where the other had been roached, and this animal carried his head menacingly low and his stud neck arched and swelled with power and with anger for the intrusion.

"That," Longarm said, "is a magnificent animal."

"It's Bucky," Catherine responded.

"I don't know. The picture I have..."

"It is Bucky, Longarm. I'm sure of it." She touched the ribs of her bay with a heel—Longarm never could understand how a woman could effectively control a horse from that ridiculous sidesaddle posture, both feet on the same side of the horse—and moved slowly forward.

The stallion raised his head and trumpeted a warning. He pawed the ground and whirled to snap at his mares and force them into a tight band before he turned to face these intruders again. His ears were pinned flat against his skull, and Longarm thought he would rather face a fistful of bank robbers than this one determined stallion if it came to a showdown.

The horse squealed again and stamped the ground.

"It's all right, Bucky. You remember me," Catherine said. Her voice was gentle and genuinely pleased. There was no tremor of fear in it.

Longarm shook his head. "I don't know Catherine. Maybe this wasn't such a good idea after all."

173

"I think you should stop your horse where you are, Long-arm, and let me go ahead alone."

"Damn it, Catherine, look at that animal. I don't know if this is the right Buck, but that animal over there sure *could* kill, if he hasn't already. Just look at him."

The stallion's neck was swollen full and his ears were still flat. The right horse or a complete stranger, this animal was more than capable of killing with teeth or heels or striking forefeet. Any animal who had to defend his mares against bears and mountain cats had to be, or he would soon be dead.

"I *know* what I am doing, Longarm. Now leave me *alone*."

Catherine handed her reins to Longarm and slid from her saddle to the ground. She walked around to the other side of her horse and rummaged in her saddlebags, all the while crooning softly to herself in a low, soothing voice.

She pulled out a small sack of corn and the halter that she used to tie her own horse. She draped the halter over her arm and poured a handful of the grain into her hand.

Palm out, showing the corn, she began to advance confidently toward the murderously angry stallion.

"Catherine, please!" He was literally begging her now. He did not want her to go anywhere near that powerful brute.

She whirled, and her eyes were flaring with a fury of her own. "Damn you, Custis Long, leave me *be*."

She turned again toward the horse and spoke to him over and over in a gentle monotone, repeating the name Bucky and steadily moving forward.

The stallion lowered his head and stamped as she came nearer. His nostrils blew wide as he snorted a warning.

"You can just quit that nonsense, Bucky. You aren't going to frighten me with your old bluff. Come on now. Come!"

She stopped and stood with her palm out, tapping her foot impatiently on the gravelly soil and demanding that the horse come to her. She was no more than ten yards from the beast now, and behind her Longarm had his hand on the stock of his Winchester. He did not want to move prematurely, afraid he might startle the stallion and make him charge her, but if the stud lunged the Winchester would be out and spitting. The only question was whether Longarm would be fast enough to keep Catherine from harm.

"Come on now, Bucky. Before you make me angry with you." She tossed a few kernels of the hard corn toward him.

One ear came up and the other was no longer so tightly pressed against the horse's magnificent head. His nostrils flared, and he lowered his head to smell the corn in front of him.

The stiffened legs bent, and the horse inched forward to stretch his thick neck and lip the ground in search of the grains. He snorted.

"There, Bucky. Isn't that better?" Catherine was smiling at the big stud. She moved toward him again, more surely this time, and tossed a few more kernels down.

Longarm wanted to shout a warning, or grab her and draw her back. But he was afraid if he moved he would only create a greater danger for her.

The second ear came up, and now both ears were tilted inquisitively toward the woman.

"You're a good boy, Bucky." She reached the horse's head.

Longarm was appalled, but damned if she didn't hold her hand out with the palm upward to let the big stud take the grain from her. Her free hand reached out to touch the horse's head.

The horse blew, kernels of corn flying, and wheeled away at her touch.

For an instant his powerful haunches were toward her, heels poised for a bone-crushing kick powerful enough to cave in the ribs of a grizzly, and Longarm's Winchester was halfway out of its boot.

"Stop that, Bucky. I'll scratch your old ears any time I want to. We already went through all that before," Catherine said calmly.

The horse allowed his ears to rise again. He turned back

to the woman and, more readily this time, moved up close against her, reaching out with his muzzle to demand more corn and nudging her with the side of his thick-jawed head.

"That's better."

Catherine fed him another handful of corn, and this time she was able to rub the buckskin's ears. She poured the rest of the bag of corn onto the ground and took her time about opening the halter.

"Raise your head, Bucky. I said raise it." She grabbed the stud firmly by one ear and yanked his muzzle away from the corn so so could slip the halter under his nose and fasten it in place.

She turned with a triumphant smile. "There you are, Longarm. Mission accomplished." She let the stud finish the grain, then led him casually to Longarm's side.

"Reckon your wild days are over, at least for a time," Longarm told the brute.

Not that he was acting in a remotely wild manner now. In Catherine Crowder's hands he was kitten-gentle.

Longarm looked up toward the sky. They had a long way to travel before they would get back down out of the mountains, and there were the mares to round up and haze along with them. Probably the best thing to do with them, Longarm thought, would be to take them all back to the store by Crystal Peak. They were all wearing brands, and their owners could reclaim them there without all the bother of a formal impoundment.

But all that would be time-consuming, and it was becoming late in the Longarm cleared his throat. "I think, ma'am, that you and I will be forced to spend another night together in camp."

Catherine smiled at him. "I don't think I will greatly mind that, Marshal Long. In fact..." She made a shockingly lewd motion with her trim hips and burst out laughing.

The woman was darn well pleased with herself, Longarm saw. Had a right to be, too. It might be a long, if pleasant, night ahead.

176

# Chapter 22

"Son of a bitch!" someone exclaimed, and Longarm grinned.

"Evening, boys. Is Brent around?" He really need not have bothered to ask. By now someone would be racing off to find the foreman of the Lazy P.

After all, it was not every evening that a deputy United States marshal came riding in on a wild killer stallion that was supposed to be shot on sight.

After all the talk, Longarm had been unable to resist the idea of putting a saddle on Buck and giving the horse a try. He had stopped on the way to the Lazy P to drift into a small herd of cattle, pointed the buckskin's nose at one in the middle, and then threw the horse the reins. The result had been satisfying gut-deep.

The horse was smooth and shifty and knew what the cow would think long before the cow had time to think it. Whatever the cow tried, Buck was there first, nose to nose with the aggravated bovine, blocking it, snapping his jaws at it, whirling with speed and precision.

Working Buck on cattle was an experience for a man to tell his grandchildren, if he had grandchildren. It was so good it would be useless for barroom conversation; no one would ever believe him. And, besides, Longarm did not know enough superlatives to explain it all. That horse could simply cut cattle the way a man might dream of but never in his life expect to see.

Longarm was glad he had done it, and if there were some questions about the regularity of it—like who owned Buck now, to give him permission to use the horse—well, there was no one around to see or to ask those questions.

Now, though, there was work to be done.

"By God, Marshal, that's him. That's old Buck as sure as I'm standing here."

"Good evening, Brent. I—uh—I reckon I did find the right horse, then."

"We thought you was going to shoot him," one of the hands said.

"That's right, Tom, but I changed my mind."

The cowboy grinned. "You're right sharp, Marshal. I didn't figure you'd remember a plain ol' cowhand like me."

Longarm smiled as he stepped down from Buck and handed the reins to the foreman. "My memory isn't always as good as it ought to be, but sooner or later I get to remembering the things I should. It comes in handy."

"Yes, sir, I reckon it would."

"For a fact."

"Is that what you came for, Marshal? To bring old Buck home?" the foreman asked.

"That's part of it. I expect he belongs here as much as anyplace, though of course you'd be doing him a favor if you were to turn him loose again. Or maybe not. I expect he'd just go to raiding homesteaders for their mares again,

178

and sooner or later somebody'd shoot him. So he'd likely be better off, and you too, if you were to keep him around and breed him. If he throws a quarter of what he is, he'd be a breeding stud to make the place some fancy money."

"I expect he would. But raidin' mares, Marshal. I thought he was in the cow-stealing business. Come to think of it, where's all the cows that have been stolen? I don't know that I want to risk tying the Lazy P up in a lot of claims and lawsuits to recover damages for all them cows Buck stole. He wouldn't be worth that to us."

"Well, there's kind of a long story behind that," Longarm said.

"You did find the cows, didn't you?"

"Not exactly."

"What'd he do, take 'em and turn 'em loose to drift? Hell, Marshal, we ought to've found some of them by now, if that was so."

"If it was so, Brent, I calculate that it would have happened just that way."

"I don't understand."

"Neither did I, for a while there. But I think I do now. I just need one more little piece of evidence and it'll all be straight."

"You can't keep that son of a bitch here, Brent," a cowboy protested. "Seeing him with a saddle on don't change the fact that he's a man-killer. You damn sure won't get me to tend him."

"Me either," someone else said.

"You boys don't have to worry about that," Longarm said.

"Marshal, you yourself seen the way Handy's skull was stove in. I'm not settin' myself up for that."

"Let me show you boys something, then. And I want you to remember, the mark was plain as plain could be on Handy's skull. He was hit with a horseshoe, right?"

"That's right, I seen it."

"Uh-huh." Longarm grinned at them. "Brent, we all trust your opinion. I'd like you to come around behind me and pick up Buck's forefeet. I'd like you to tell me what you see there."

The truth was that the foreman was the only one of the crowd that Longarm would trust behind his back. But there was no point in making an issue of that. Not quite yet.

"Why, the old bastard is barefoot, Marshal. Wore down a little, too. He could use a set o' plates on him or he'll get sore-footed."

"That's right, Brent. Like any other horse that runs loose, his shoes came off after a while. You can tell by the shape of his hoof that he hasn't been wearing shoes for quite some time now."

"But..."

"Buck isn't your killer, Brent. That's about what it comes down to. This old boy has been up in the high country near good grass and cold-flowing water, like any sensible horse would be. That's where I found him, three days ago. Had him a little bunch of mares he'd stolen from some folks up there, and he was happy as a pig in the sunshine."

"You mean we got *another* killer horse running loose around here?"

Longarm's answering smile held no humor in it. He was tight-lipped and grim. "I wouldn't exactly say that either, Brent. But I do think you've got a killer running loose. Of the two-legged variety."

"I don't understand."

"Two of these boys here do."

"Two of *my* boys?"

Longarm shook his head. He was staring at the men, not at the foreman. "Not any more, Brent. Those sons of bitches are mine now. It will take me about five minutes to figure out which ones they are. Then them and me are going to take a train ride. There are some Federal charges they have to answer to in Denver."

He could feel tension building in the men. There were eight or nine of them in the group, and they began to look at one another uneasily.

Slowly, almost as if they did not realize what they were

180

doing, the Lazy P hands began to separate, drifting apart from each other.

"Don't be taking off on me now, boys. I wouldn't take kindly to that," Longarm said.

The certainty in Longarm's voice was too much for Tom Morris to take. He clawed for the revolver at his belt.

Longarm's Colt spoke first, and Morris went down with a bullet in his chest. It was over before some of the men realized it had begun.

The sweet, fresh odor of burnt black powder hung in the air, and the memory of the sound of the gunshot was heavy.

"I suggest that Tom's partner, whichever of you it is, gives up now," Longarm said. "I'm going to find you anyhow. I don't want to have to shoot you too."

"Aw, shit, Marshal, it's a hangin' offense anyhow."

"It is that, old son."

The cowboy went for his gun. This time the crowd had parted when he began to speak, and the men were watching as he grabbed the butt of his rusting Smith and Wesson and tried to get it out of the confinement of his holster.

He was too far away to buffalo, and Longarm had no choice. The heavy Colt, already in his hand, barked again, and a slug took the cowboy in the stomach.

"I think that's all of them, Brent, but I'll have to make sure." Longarm was watching the remaining men as he spoke, but none of them flinched or tried to avoid his gaze. For the most part they looked confused and uncertain, but there was no hint of guilty knowledge on any of their faces.

Longarm sighed and began to reload his Colt. It was over. Or almost.

A search of the bunkhouse turned up the evidence he expected to find there. In Tom Morris's slicker was a short, sturdy club with a horseshoe nailed to its wickedly blunt end.

"That's what killed those men," Longarm said. "It wasn't any horse; it was that club leaving a print to put the blame on old Buck."

"But . . ."

"The cows? That was almost the easy part, once I got over assuming that it was a horse running those cattle off. It had to be people, and their reason had to be money. Those cattle were stolen and sold and butchered and eaten."

"How? Everybody around here knows the brands those cattle were wearing. You couldn't sell them just anyplace."

"Oh, you couldn't sell them in Fountain or in Monument. Like you say, everybody knows the brands and would have wanted some proof of ownership before they'd buy a beef wearing the wrong brand.

"But I got to thinking about two things. One, no one around here is willing to do business with those high-hat Easterners over in Colorado Springs. You just won't trade with them."

"Damn right we won't."

"The other thing is, those businessmen over there *are* Easterners. They don't know shit from green apples when it comes to our way of doing things.

"Yet a little while back I was served an awful fine piece of fresh grass-fed beef in the Antlers Hotel over there. Eventually I got to thinking about that. It took longer than it should have, but eventually I worked it out. So a few days ago I had a talk with the chef at the hotel and then another talk with the fella who supplies beef to him. The butcher's a German. Doesn't hardly speak English, much less know about brands.

"It seems there's been a couple young cowboys driving in three or four head at a time to sell to him whenever he needs fresh beef to slaughter. He was happy as hell about the deal. Never paid any mind to the scars on the critters, of course. He was just glad to get the beef without having to pay to ship it down from Denver. Over a period of months it amounted to a right heavy traffic. Enough that those boys didn't want anyone finding out it wasn't Buck that was stealing the cattle. That's why they hired a rifleman to kill those two government hunters who were after Buck and then to make a try at me when I was doing the same thing.

"It was worth it to them to kill whenever some home-

182

steader caught them at it. By doing it with that club instead of a gun, they helped their own cause too, by putting the blame more solidly on old Buck." Longarm shrugged. "It worked. You don't argue with success."

Brent shook his head. "I still can't hardly believe it. I worked side by side with those boys for quite a while. But why in hell did they have to kill Handy? They weren't trying to steal anything then."

"We'll never know for sure," Longarm said. "But probably they realized that Handy was no pilgrim. It wouldn't have taken him near as long as it did me to figure out that no wild horse was going to be down here when it could be up in the cool country. So they killed him and hoped I'd be too dumb to figure it out on my own. That part didn't work. Though if I'd been quicker to start thinking and quit just reacting, maybe Handy and some other good people wouldn't have been killed."

"Shit," Brent mouthed. He pulled a chew from his back pocket, offered Longarm a bite from it, and took one himself when Longarm refused.

"You don't think that Buck horse is a killer, then?" one of the men asked.

"Lew Chance is dead enough, but I'd guess it was just an unlucky accident that he was kicked in the head when he got bucked off that time."

The man nodded. He seemed satisfied. An accident with a rough horse was something he faced every time he climbed into the saddle of a range-bred working horse.

"I don't suppose you need me around here as a reminder," Longarm said. "I have to get going. I have to take those bodies into town and get that German butcher to identify them for me."

He did not add that by then he would have missed his train back to Denver. The bodies could wait on ice until morning.

And in the meantime there was a widow not far away whose company wasn't bad, even if she didn't serve any meat at her table.

Watch for

LONGARM AND THE CALICO KID

fifty-fourth novel in the bold
LONGARM series from Jove

*coming in April!*

# LONGARM

Explore the exciting Old West with
one of the men who made it wild!

# LONGARM

Explore the exciting Old West with
one of the men who made it wild!